Fr

A Stranded Novel

By Theresa Shaver

Contents

Author's Note

Hello! Back in the saddle again after a prolonged break between books. Huge thanks to you all for sticking with me. I know many of you are waiting for the third book in Endless Winter, Sun & Smoke, me too! It IS coming, I promise. Sometimes you just have to go with the flow and write what's in your head. I thought I was pretty much done with the Stranded series but this story line kept nagging and nagging to be told. What would the teens do over that first cold winter? After a horrible early winter with three weeks of -35C here, I felt like a prisoner in my own house. Even with plowed roads, seat warmers in the car and the furnace cranked up. It was like a pardon was given to my sentence when the weather finally broke and a Chinook rolled in pushing temperatures up to above freezing! I couldn't help but think about how we could survive that without modern conveniences. So, Frozen, book 5 came about. I was adamant that this would finally be the last book in the series... Why won't this book end???!!! I was writing and writing and people were asking, "Are you done yet?" And I was writing and writing... It finally took my too smart for her age 9-year-old, saying one night at dinner, "Maybe you're not done because it's going to be 2 books!" for me to realize that, yes, it will have to be 2 books. So Iced, book six will be written.

I now have both Iced, a Stranded Novel and Sun & Smoke in the works and I'm just going to let it flow. That means I'm not sure which one will come next.

I have to say a HUGE thank you to all of you for the amazing reviews you leave and for all the comments and letters asking for more. Keep them coming!

Also, to my sweet husband and children who encourage me every day. I couldn't do any of this without you.

Xoxo
Theresa

Chinook
shi-noo k, -nook

*A chinook, (meaning "snow-eater") is a warm dry
southwesterly wind blowing down the eastern slopes of the
Rocky Mountains capable of creating drastic temperature
increases in short periods of time.*

Prologue

The man stumbled under the weight of his trade goods as he reached the bottom of the stairs leading up into the community center where the market day was in full swing. He paused to catch his breath but the many scarves protecting his face from the bitter Alberta cold felt like they were strangling him, so he ripped them down with a shaking hand. A deep breath of frigid air had his fever-wracked body shaking so hard he almost lost his footing. Tired and burning eyes lifted to the doors at the top of the stairs with the hope that he might find the medicine he and his family needed to beat back the bug that they had all caught.

He cursed the travelers he had traded with that had brought the germ to his doorstep. At the time, he hadn't thought much about the coughing they all seemed afflicted with because he was eager to have the bottles of booze they wanted to trade for food. Alcohol was in short supply eight months after the event that had shut the lights off and he knew he could make some fantastic deals with it at the market. Now he just hoped he could use the booze to trade for medicine.

He had just made it to the doors and pushed them open when the first agonizing cough hit him. It was so severe that he didn't even see the group of people leaving the market and he crashed into them all. With his scarves pulled down, the germs infecting his body were free to spread to them all with every cough. As blackness closed in, the last thing he heard was the sound of the liquor bottles in his bag hitting the floor and glass smashing.

Manny people in the market turned at the sound and rushed to help the ailing man. As hard as the recent months had been on the people of Prairie Springs, they all had a great sense of community. That made it even easier for the plague to spread.

Chapter One

Alex squeezed her eyes tight and burrowed deeper under the covers when a shift by Dara beside her in the bed opened a small gap and allowed the cold air in the room to trickle down her back. More than anything, Alex wanted to keep the warmth around her for as long as she could. First thing in the morning upon waking was the only moment of her day that she felt truly warm.

She tried to fade back into the peacefulness of sleep but it was too late. Her brain had clicked on and the anger and sadness soon followed. The cold was numbing and miserable but she thought she could handle it if everything else hadn't gone so wrong. She squirmed even deeper under the covers as Dara got up to throw a thick piece of wood into the modified stove at the center of the room before hurrying back to the warmth of the bed. They had developed a routine where they took turns each day to get the fire going again and the room heated up before they even attempted to get out of bed and dressed for the day.

It had been almost nine months since the lights went out. It seemed like forever ago that she and her friends had set off from Disneyland on the epic journey to get home to Canada. They all suffered the internal scars from what they had been forced to do on the trip and the battle of rescuing their town from a gang that had taken it over.

Ironically, it was because of what the gang had forced the townspeople to do that they were in such good shape halfway through the winter. The gang had emptied every pantry, grocery store and cellar of food and stored it in the community center while forcing the townspeople to plant crops in fields and gardens in every park in town. They had been put on starvation rations causing many of them to drop unhealthy weight they had been carrying around on their bodies. By the time Alex and her friends had helped rescue them they were all abused and tired but many were also the healthiest they had been in years. With all the food in town in one location, the newly formed town council was able to stretch the rations out until the first crops were ready to harvest. As sad and traumatic as the town's takeover had been, they were all able to continue working together after they had their freedom to ensure a bumper harvest. Something that most likely would not have happened if they hadn't been forced to work by gunpoint.

It was glorious to be home safe with their families, but all the teens had changed from the actions they were forced to take to make it home and then free the town. Unfortunately, their parents and families had a hard time accepting these changes and they became fiercely overprotective. New restrictions were placed on the teens that they had never dealt with before. Alex tugged the covers higher over her head and let her mind drift back to the end of summer and the last time she really felt happy.

****

Alex jumped down from the wagon almost before it came to a stop. She raced to the back and grabbed the huge bag of buns that she had baked as her contribution to the harvest party being held on Quinn's grandparent's farm. She couldn't wait to see her friends and catch up. It felt like it had been forever since they had all been together.

With most of the harvesting being done by hand, the sheer amount of work has left little time for socializing. Add to that the restrictions that her parents had put on her movements since she had gotten back from California and that meant she hardly ever saw anyone anymore if they weren't working on her family's farm. She understood in her heart why her parents wanted her close by, but after years of being able to roam around the woods and her friend's properties as well as the trip home, she was starting to really resent being treated like a child. She was trusted with more responsibilities on the farm than a lot of the adults that were there to work as field hands, but she wasn't allowed to cross a few fields to visit with her friends. She might be a teenage girl in years but she was an adult in so many other ways.

Alex ignored the other people climbing down from the wagon and pretended not to hear her mom when she called out to her to stay close by.

"Really? Where am I going to go except across the yard?" she thought sarcastically.

Alex dashed through the growing crowd towards the barn where lines of tables were already groaning under the weight of so many bowls, pots and platters of food. After the last few months of carefully controlled portions, everyone was going to enjoy the rewards of the harvest at tonight's feast. She found an empty spot on a table and placed her bag of buns on it before she whirled around and started scanning the crowd for her friends. Josh's huge bellow of laughter had her darting around the side of the barn and following it to the yard behind.

Her feet slid to a stop as a grin split across her face. There they were. Josh had David in a headlock as they stumbled around in a circle while Emily, Dara and Lisa stood together rolling their eyes and laughing at them. It was so good to see her friends but her eyes locked on to the one she missed the most and her feet carried her across the floor to him. Quinn caught her up in his arms and swung her around before settling her back on her feet and resting his forehead against hers. They just stood there staring into each other's eyes until Josh started making kissing and moaning sounds. The finally broke apart with grins on their faces and turned to their friends.

"Ugh, I thought you guys were gonna ogle each other all night! Come on! Let's get this party started!" Josh teased.

"Hey, try ogling with your own girlfriend and it might be a party for YOU!" Dara poked at him.

Josh dramatically fell to his knees and clasped his hands in front of his heart.

"Oh, love of my life, I do solemnly vow to ogle you all night long once the sun has set and the music starts but most

~ 9 ~

importantly, NOT until I've filled me starving belly at least twice!"

Everyone was laughing as Dara shook her head in exasperation. "How did I ever end up with such a romantic idiot like you?" she asked mockingly.

"Epic cosmic lottery win?"

Trying to hold back her laughter, Dara hauled Josh to his feet, planted a kiss on him and started dragging him back around the barn to the food tables. Everyone else followed but Quinn held Alex back until they were alone.

"Man, I miss you. I can't stand knowing you're across a few fields but we still hardly see each other!" he told her.

Alex groaned, "I know. My parents are driving me crazy. If I'm out of sight for more than ten minutes they start to get frantic with worry! I don't know how much more of their overprotectiveness I can take. I just want some space and the freedoms I used to have. It's like they don't think I can take care of myself anymore!"

Quinn tugged on one of her loose red gold curls before tucking it behind her ear.

"My grandparents aren't quite so bad but even they're keeping me close to home. I get how worried they were when we were gone but I think we proved just how capable we all are." He sighed and pulled her closer. "I miss you and I want to be with you. With winter coming it'll only get harder for us to be together so I have something to ask you." Quinn took a deep breath before continuing. "We've known each other almost our whole lives and I think I've loved you for just as long. We've been through so much together in the last few months. The world is such a different place now and we've learned that anything can happen in an instant. I want us to be happy and grab as much life as we can. Your birthday is next month and then we'll both be eighteen. So...Alex, will you marry me?"

Alex's mouth dropped open in shock but it only lasted for an instant before it turned into a face-splitting smile. She threw herself against him and yelled out, "YES, yes, yes, yes!"

None of the old-world restrictions mattered anymore. She knew this boy, this man, and she loved him with every fiber of her being. They had all seen how quickly things could change and go bad. Grabbing a chance at happiness was all that mattered.

Quinn slipped a small ring on her finger and with love and hope on their faces went to share the news with their families and friends.

There were a lot of mixed reactions to their announcement. Of course, their friends all cheered and congratulated them, but Alex's parents were a different story. Her dad frowned and her mom started shaking her head immediately.

"No, no kids. I know you think you love each other but you're both WAY too young to really know what that means! You're just kids."

Quinn's grandmother tried a different tact. "Perhaps a long engagement would be best? That way you could really be sure and a few years down the road we could talk about it again."

Harry Dennison was the only adult that showed any kind of support. He looked closely at both of their faces and saw what the others didn't. Love, happiness and determination. He started nodding and held up one huge hand to quiet the other adults before speaking.

"You both have always been more mature than average teenagers your age. We all trust you and give you great responsibilities on the farm so it's only fair that we trust you in this as well. After all, Anna and I got married when she was only seventeen and that seemed to work out just fine."

Alice Andrews, Alex's mom, jumped in at that. "Oh, Harry, that was a different time!"

Harry chuckled, "Take a look around, Alice, we are back in that time. Things have reversed back to when I was a young man. This new world is very unpredictable and they deserve a shot at happiness."

The adults continued to argue so Alex and Quinn slipped away and joined their friends at another table after grabbing heaping plates of food from the buffet. Josh started laying out plans as soon as they sat down.

"You'll need a place of your own but it's too late to start building before the cold hits and I'm sure you don't want to spend the winter in the tree house. I think we should haul over one of the nicer campers from the RV storage yard at the resort. We can insulate the crap out of it, skirt the underside and then frame up a carport shelter over it. We've got over a hundred bottles of propane that we kept back from what we took from the resort so that's our wedding gift to you guys. That should keep you in heat for the winter. BUT, you have to let us come hang out in your new clubhouse once the cold hits with the heat on high!"

They spent the rest of the party eating, dancing and making plans for the future. It was the last time Alex truly felt happiness.

Tears trickled from the corners of her eyes and onto her pillow at the sad memories that came next.

She had woken up the morning after the harvest party with joy in her heart and dressed quickly to go meet her friends. They planned on going to the RV resort to pick out her and Quinn's new home. She was ready for her parent's objections but was planning on going anyway. It was time they understood she wasn't a child anymore. When she ran down the stairs and entered the kitchen she wasn't surprised to see her parents waiting for her at the kitchen table. She just didn't expect to see the tears pouring down her mother's face or the deep lines of grief etched into her dad's.

"Alex, honey, come sit down. We have some sad news to tell you." her dad said.

Once she was seated they both reached over and clasped hands with her.

"I'm so sorry sweetheart, Quinn's grandfather passed away last night. I know how much Harry meant to you."

Alex shook her head. "What are you talking about? He was fine last night at the party. He even danced with me!"

Her dad pulled her into a one-armed hug. "I know. He had a great time at the party but once everyone left, Anna says he sat down in his rocker on the porch and fell asleep and he passed away. It was very peaceful for him."

Tears started pouring down her face as a hundred memories of Harry rushed through her mind. That man had been in her life since the day she was born and had treated her like a granddaughter. She was devastated and couldn't even imagine how Quinn must be feeling. Harry had taken on the role of father to Quinn when his son and daughter-in-law had died. She had to go to him.

Alex pulled away from her parents and jumped to her feet. "I have to go. I have to go to Quinn."

She left her parents there and raced out of the house. She ignored the people standing around in the yard that were there to help with the work of putting food and wood up for the coming winter. She had one goal and it was to get to Quinn as quickly as possible. That meant burning some carefully rationed gas. Where normally they walked or took the horse drawn wagon anywhere they needed to go, today she didn't care. It only took seconds to fire up one of the farm's ATVs and head out across the field towards Quinn's place. By the time she hit the edge of the barnyard she had managed to get her tears under control.

It was no surprise to see many wagons, horses and other ATVs already parked around the barn. Harry Dennison was a pillar of the community and it was due to his experience and cool head that a lot of people had survived the event that changed everything. He would be greatly missed by all.

When Alex shut her machine off, she heard the sound of another racing towards her. Seconds later, Josh came to a halt and parked next to her. His face was pale and tears leaked down his face. As much as Josh was a goof, he had the biggest heart of them all. He didn't say anything as he dismounted and pulled her into a bear hug, making her own tears surge back. He finally let her go and cleared his throat.

"Have you seen him yet?"

Alex couldn't speak through the sob in her throat so she just shook her head. Josh took her arm and the headed towards the house but the sound of an axe hitting wood had them veering around to the backside of the barn. That's where they found Quinn. He was only wearing a drenched in sweat t-shirt, despite the cool morning air, as he poured his emotions into destroying each piece of wood. They waited patiently for him to acknowledge them, but minutes passed as he just kept swinging the axe. Josh finally stepped towards him.

"Quinn, you should ease up, man. You're going to hurt yourself."

Neither Josh nor Alex was prepared for the rage filled eyes that lifted up to meet theirs. His voice was filled with bitter anger.

"His pills ran out two weeks ago. All they had to do was tell me and I could have gone looking for more! That stubborn bastard held out until after the harvest was in and then just left. He left Grams and me here alone to do this by ourselves! How could he do that? How am I supposed to take over for him?"

Alex rushed towards him, stunned by his harsh words but knowing it was the grief talking.

"Quinn, Quinn don't say that! Harry would never leave you willingly and you're not alone. I'm here and Josh and the others, plus the whole town will be here to help too."

Quinn evaded her outstretched hands and spun away.

"Just leave me alone, Alex. You have no idea what you're talking about!"

Josh had come up right behind Alex and he tried to reason with his best friend.

"Come on Quinn, you know we're all here for you. I'm sorry about Harry, he was a great man and it'll be hard to fill his shoes but we'll all work together. We'll all be here for you and your Grams."

Quinn made a strangled bellow of rage before turning and throwing the axe overhand towards the barn. The blade bit into the wood halfway up the wall, quivering from the force of the throw.

"Just leave me the hell alone!"

Alex and Josh stood in disbelief and watched as Quinn stalked away towards the woods. Neither of them had ever seen him display anything more than mild anger before. This violent rage was completely opposite of his personality.

Josh finally tugged Alex away and they headed towards the house to pay their respects to Harry's wife, Anna.

"He'll be ok. It's just the grief hitting him. Give him some time to come to terms with it Alex."

All she could do was nod her head and hope that Josh was right.

Chapter Two

It seemed that the death of Harry Dennison was a trigger that started a chain reaction of bad things to come. The day after he was laid to rest, the weather turned and freezing temperatures and snow blanketed the town. No one could ever remember winter coming so early before and most believed that it was the effects of nuclear winter. It became obvious after the first week that people wouldn't be able to heat all the homes being occupied, so families were forced to triple up to conserve heat.

Alex's family home was a large sprawling farmhouse with four wood burning fireplaces and a pellet stove. Her dad had switched the backup generator for the house to propane a few years back, but had kept an old trailer mounted diesel generator in running condition as well that they could use for the outbuildings if needed. They ran them off and on when they needed a boost of heat from the furnace or pellet stove, or to pump up water from the well. A large propane tank supplied the backup generator for the house and the furnace, but that had to be conserved as much as possible to make sure they made it through the winter. Wood burning stoves were created from old barrels and then installed with exhaust ducts in almost every room to help heat the home.

The sound of wood-chopping and chainsaws filled every minute of the waning daylight for weeks as they prepared to stock enough to survive the cold winter to come. In between wood gathering details, the teens helped scavenge old parts for Josh as he worked on getting snowmobiles running. They had spent a lot of winters in the past sledding for fun, so each family in their group had at least two machines in their barns or sheds but some of the newer models were filled with electronics and completely dead. They knew they would be stuck in place once the roads became deep with snow and they all wanted to be able to travel at least to each other's farms.

Alex's house filled up with more people than had ever lived in it. Dara and her little brother Jake had been living in the camper the teens had brought back from California. It had kept them comfortably over the summer, but the dropping temperatures were too much so she and Jake moved into to Alex's room for the winter.

Alex's brother Peter, his wife Susan, and their newborn baby arrived the day after the first snowfall. They were a welcome addition to the home and Alex's parents were thrilled to have all of their family safely under their roof.

Not so welcome was the family assigned to them from town. It had been agreed to at a town meeting that families doubling and tripling up would bring supplies to share and help with the many chores it now took to survive a single day without modern conveniences. A single woman and her three little boys were assigned to stay with them for the duration of the winter. The mother's name was Jessie and she brought bags of dirty clothes, three undisciplined boys under the age of eight and lots of complaints.

With seven adults, four little boys and one baby crammed into her house, Alex was ready to break by the first week of December. Quinn had pretty much stopped talking to her and the rest of their friends and with the weather being so harsh, they were practically trapped on the property, causing her own rage to build day by day. Her life seemed to only consist of farm chores, kitchen chores, laundry chores and trying not to freeze any parts on her body. She never seemed to have any space or time alone and it was taking its toll.

When the first week of December passed with no one mentioning the holidays, Alex woke up determined to have some cheer back in her life. As she helped wash the breakfast dishes one morning with her mom, she brought it up.

"Mom, why don't we stay inside today and put up all the Christmas decorations? Dad and Peter could go cut us a tree. It would be nice to have some fun for a change."

Before Alice Andrews could reply, Jessie, who was sitting in her customary seat beside the fireplace doing her thousandth Sudoku puzzle jumped in.

"Oh my God, can we have pie? I'd kill for pie. I'm so sick of all the plain food we eat here!"

Alex clenched her teeth and kept silent, determined to keep her hopeful mood alive for one day.

Alice set the dish she was drying down on the counter and turned to reply to the woman in a very neutral tone.

"I'm sorry you don't enjoy my cooking Jessie. Perhaps you could cook a meal for everyone tonight?"

Jessie scrunched up her nose before turning back to her puzzle. "No, that's ok. I just meant you could add in some spices or something sometimes. It just gets a little bland, you know?"

Alice turned back to the sink and picked up another dish to dry. Alex glanced at her from the corner of her eye and saw her mom was trying very hard not to answer the woman. She finally looked her way and smiled.

"Yes, let's do that. I think everyone could use a little holiday cheer. We can decorate the house and plan to have a special Christmas meal…with pie."

Mother and daughter shared a knowing smile with each other but were interrupted by a crash of breaking glass from the living room followed by the sounds of yelling boys that almost drowned out the sudden wail of a baby crying.

They both turned quickly away from the sink to see what had happened now with the young terrors living in their home but were stopped in their tracks by Jessie's screech.

"Oh my God! I can't concentrate with all this racket!" Her frustrated face turned towards them and she snapped, "Alex, go play with those boys and get them settled down!"

Last straw, last, final, done was all Alex could think. All the hope she had for a better day vanished as red fury filled her vision.

"ARE YOU KIDDING ME? Who the hell do you think you are? You come into our home and contribute nothing,

NOTHING! You sit there day after day for over a month now doing your stupid puzzles while the rest of us cook, clean and serve you. Your three brats run wild with no supervision by you and they wreck everything they touch and all you do is COMPLAIN! I am not your nanny. Get off your lazy butt and take care of them yourself!"

Alex was so filled with fury from all that had happened since the lights went out and she finally found an outlet for her anger. She had no idea that she was screaming at the top of her lungs and that everyone in the house was rushing to the kitchen when Jessie snarled back at her.

"How dare you talk to me with such disrespect? You have no idea how hard it was for me and the boys when the power went out! Those monsters came here and treated us like cattle. They taunted us and barely fed us every day. It was traumatizing! I'm sorry if me escaping into my "stupid" puzzles bothers you, but it's my way of coping with what I went through."

Alex didn't see her father, brother or Dara come into the room. All she could see was the weak pathetic excuse for a person who wanted her to feel sorry for her.

"What a trauma!" she said sarcastically. "You had to sit in a gym with a little bit less food and have people be mean to you. Boo hoo, poor you! Do you have any idea what's out there in the real world? I crossed a country never knowing each day if I would live or die to the next one. I had a biker gang hang me on a wall by hooks so they could rape me and then I was forced to kill them all just to live another day. I had to cut open my boyfriend's body and dig bullets out of it not knowing if it would kill him or save him. And then! Then, I finally get home and find my family enslaved and AGAIN, I'm forced to kill more people. I've seen heaps of dead bodies of people I knew and liked thrown away like garbage and girls I used to go to school with used for their bodies. So, tell me again just how TRAUMATIZED you are!"

Her chest was heaving at the raw emotion finally flowing out of it as a whimpering Jessie fled the room. It felt so good to get some of the pain out but it left her weak in the knees and feeling like she needed to vomit. Her eyes met Dara's across the room and she saw the same feelings mirrored in her friend's eyes. No one could understand what they'd been through and it was all still there bubbling under the surface.

"Alex, did that really happen? My God baby, why didn't you tell us?" Her mother asked in a tortured whisper as she reached out a shaking hand to her little girl.

Alex, swallowed hard and shoved tears from her cheeks and then gave a sharp nod.

"I'm sorry, you didn't need to know that. It's in the past and I'd like to leave it there."

Her father's face was bone white with grief and shock as he stepped towards her.

"Alex, we can't just forget about it. We need to talk about this. You need to tell us everything sweetheart."

Alex felt like a trapped bird and her eyes flew around the room looking for an escape route as she quickly shook her head. No, she couldn't talk to them about it, not now, maybe never. It was just the anger at that woman that made her even speak of it. Her brother quickly stepped between her and her dad and grabbed her by the shoulders. His face was firm and understanding.

"No, you don't need to talk about it. Not now, if you want to one day then we can but you don't need to do it today. Go, go on out and get some air. Dara will go with you. I'll… I will talk to Mom and Dad. Everything is ok, Alex. Go on, little sister."

Alex could barely contain the sob of relief that was growing in her chest as she turned away from her big brother and flew around her mom to the back door. Her feet dropped into her boots and her hand snagged her jacket as she shoved the door open to the frigid cold. The bitter air slapped her in the face as she struggled to pull her jacket on and get control of her breathing. She was furious and so sad all at the same time. She didn't know what to do or where to go so she just stood there. Faint sounds of raised voices came from inside the house. She heard her brother's voice yelling something about PTSD and it caused all the anger to drain away and shame to replace it. All she had wanted was a happy day where she didn't have to think about everything that had happened in the last six months. Instead, she brought heartache and pain to her loved ones.

After ten minutes the door behind her opened and slammed closed, causing her to flinch. It filled her with relief when it was Dara who walked around her. She stood like a child as her friend dressed her in a toque, scarf and mittens.

"Dara, I just…"

Dara shook her head. "Come on, it's too cold out here. Let's go fire up the motorhome and burn some propane."

The girls walked across the yard to where the camper that had brought them home and gave them shelter was parked. There were snow banks piled high around three sides of it leaving the side door and exhaust pipe cleared. Even though Dara and Jake had moved into the house once the real cold had hit, she had been keeping it clear of snow and running it for a few minutes every day to keep it operational. Alex wasn't the only one that needed a little space from all the people crammed into the house.

The girls settled into the small dinette and sat in silence as the air slowly warmed around them from the blowing propane furnace. Once it was warm enough to remove their hats, scarves and mittens, Dara reached over and grasped Alex's hand.

"It's ok to feel this way. All of us are messed up from what happened on the trip. I don't think any of us has really talked about everything that happened."

Alex lowered her eyes and let out a breath. "How am I supposed to talk to them about all that? They still see their little girl when they look at me. That's not who I am anymore! The things I saw, the things I've…done, have changed me." Alex looked around the small space inside the camper and shook her head. "We fought so hard to get back here and free our people but all I really want now is to drive this camper out of here and run away. As scary as the trip was, I MISS us, I miss all of us being together, being a team that just plows ahead and gets what needs to be done, done."

Dara nodded, "Yeah, I miss it too. I mean, I'm happy to not have bullets flying my way and knowing Jake is safe is a huge relief but I miss our team and being with them all." She peered through the frosted window towards the house in thought before turning back to Alex. "I think this is why soldiers do it. Why they keep re-enlisting for tour after tour. Having a team, having a mission, it's like it gives them a more meaningful reason to get up every day. We were soldiers for a while there and now we just go through the motions of living each day. It kind of feels empty."

"That's exactly how I feel! Now there's so much time that I think about everything that happened way too much. I wake up angry, I go to bed angry and it just seems to get worse every day! I need... I need to do something but I don't know what to do! It makes it even harder to deal, with all of us spread out and hardly seeing each other. Add in Quinn basically dumping me the day after he asked me to marry him and I'm ready to shoot someone. It's probably a good thing that we hid away most of the guns we brought back or I'd have probably shot that woman this morning!" Alex joked.

Dara smirked, "Well, I don't think you have to worry about her anymore. Your dad's taking her and her kids back into town this afternoon. They'll find another family to take them in and we'll probably get some others. After you left the house, he said he'd had enough of them. I guess he'd already been putting out feelers to move them before the big blowout today."

Alex sighed in frustration. "I'm glad they're going but I'm sorry I blew up like that. How am I supposed to go in there now and answer all the questions they'll have?"

Dara shook her head. "You don't and you won't have to. Your brother's a pretty smart guy. He told them to leave you alone about this. He said you probably have PTSD and will need time to work through it. He told them that you might never tell them everything that happened and that they would need to be ok with that. He's seen it before with a few guys on the force. He also told them that they need to loosen the reins a little and let you have more freedom to move around so that should help some."

Alex closed her eyes and sent a grateful prayer up for Peter, for him being here and for his understanding. When she opened them and met Dara's, she felt a huge weight come off her shoulders. She was also very grateful for her. Emily had always been her best friend but Dara was just as important to her now and she needed to trust her with something she had been keeping secret from everyone.

"How do you feel about getting out of here and going for a drive?" Alex asked her.

Dara shrugged and grinned. "If your mom is ok watching Jake then I'm happy to get away for a while. Where do you want to go?"

A grin split across Alex's face, "Christmas shopping!"

Chapter Three

Alex wasn't ready to face her parents yet so Dara went into the house and asked about Jake and if they could go for a ride to see some of their other friends. She left the house with Alex's parent's permission and a shotgun that Alex's dad insisted they take for "just in case". She also brought out extra snow gear that they would need to wear to protect themselves from the extreme cold.

Alex wouldn't tell Dara where they were going and she decided that riding the horses would take too long and the extreme cold wouldn't be good for them so she backed out one of the two working snowmobiles her family owned from the garage and waved Dara to climb on. They took off across the fields and enjoyed being away from the farm for the first time in weeks. Alex drove the ski-doo with the confidence of someone who has been riding and driving for years. She had learned how to ride a dirt bike at eleven and never looked back. One of the best things about growing up on a farm was that most of them had learned how to drive various machines earlier than most kids.

They made it to their destination quickly and she drove around to the back side of a house before parking and turning the machine off. Once the girls were inside the dim abandoned house, Dara looked around in confusion.

"Whose place is this and where's the extra seasonal help to wrap all the Christmas presents I'll be buying?"

Alex laughed as she pulled one thick glove off and ran a finger through the layer of dust on a side table.

"It's Mrs. Moore's house and you can wrap your own gifts this year."

The girls walked over to the fireplace mantle and studied the dusty pictures of their teacher and her family.

"Do you think she's still alive?" Dara asked sadly.

Alex gave a firm nod. "Oh yeah, I have no doubts about that at all. I'm not so sure about some of our classmates that stayed behind but Mrs. Moore will make it home. She'll be here no later than the end of summer which is why what I'm about to show you is so important. Follow me."

Alex led Dara down the basement steps, pulling a flashlight out of her pocket and lighting the way. With the snow outside covering all the basement windows, it was almost pitch black down there. She started explaining to Dara as they went down the stairs.

"You know how prepared Mrs. Moore was that day in Disneyland. She knew almost right away what had happened and what we had to do to survive. She's been planning for something like this to happen for years. She told me a few things just in case she doesn't make it home, but I truly believe she'll get here." Alex stopped in the middle of the small room at the bottom of the stairs and turned to Dara with a serious face. "We're doing pretty well right now at home as far as supplies go. We have everything that we really need to survive even if we don't have a lot of the luxuries we used to. The thing is, once certain things are all used up then they're gone for good, so that makes everything so much more precious and we need to be very careful to make stuff last as long as possible."

Dara raised her eyebrows in a "DUH" expression. "I'm well aware of that Alex. I know I won't be hitting the mall anytime soon. What exactly are we here for?"

Alex bit her lip in hesitation before saying, "I trust you but I just need you to promise me that you won't tell anyone, like ANYONE, aka Josh, about what I'm going to show you."

Dara held up her hand in a mock oath taking way and pledged, "I, Dara Langston, do solemnly swear not to tell ANYONE, including Josh, what I'm about to see. I swear this on my membership in the Maple Leaf Mafia!"

Alex cracked up with laughter and threw her hands up, causing the flashlight beam to bounce around the room. "Ok, ok already!" She then turned and popped open the secret door built into the wall, reached around the doorframe and snagged a lantern that she had left there the last time she was here and moved further into the room turning on more lanterns until it was well lit.

Dara stood in the doorway with her mouth gaping open and her eyes scanning the rows of shelving piled high with supplies. She started shaking her head in disbelief until her eyes zeroed in on a particular shelf.

"Holy Mother Mary and Joseph! Is that Kraft dinner? Seriously? Is that one, two, three…Oh my God, ten cases of Kraft dinner! Alex, I will give you anything for just one box. One box from ten cases isn't so much, pleeeease?"

Alex was laughing and it felt like the first real laugh she'd had in months. "Yup, you can have a box but really Dara, out of all this, why a simple box of KD?"

Dara had moved into the room to get a better look at what was piled up but she walked straight to the cases she wanted and ran a hand over them.

"It's just sometimes Jake and I didn't have a lot of food in the house when Mom was on a real bender, but I could always scrounge around enough change to buy a box or two of it. It's comfort food, you know? It always made us happy to have it."

Alex nodded in understanding. "I'm sorry you guys had it so hard. I wish I had of known."

Dara waved away her concern. "Don't worry about it. Things are so much better for us now that we live with your family. Hey, who knew the apocalypse would make Jake and my lives' better!" Dara turned away and started looking at everything else. "How on earth have you been sitting on this for so long without telling anyone, or eating it all for that matter?"

Alex walked over to the small desk in the corner and pulled the sheets of inventory out of a drawer.

"Mrs. Moore was pretty clear on how to use this stuff if we needed too. She really hammered home that this stuff is last resort. It can't be replaced, and being a little hungry from small portions and rationing isn't an emergency, but having no food left and no way to get more is. All of this needs to stay put as a last resort. Can you imagine how fast this would be gone if people knew it was here? No, this is definitely worst case scenario back up food. I know it's tempting but it needs to stay here. BUT…I'd like to think Mrs. Moore wouldn't mind if we took just a couple things for Christmas presents."

Dara was scanning the inventory pages and nodding her head. "You're totally right. This is the backup for absolute starvation. I can tell you it makes me feel better to know it's here if something awful happens." She lifted her eyes from the pages with concern. "Are you sure we should take anything from here? We are doing ok right now. It does seem like there's a lot here but it would go pretty fast if we take some now and again. Maybe we shouldn't."

A slow smile came across Alex's face as she pulled a second, larger stack of sheets from the drawer and handed them to Dara. "I knew you were the right person to tell. You get how important this could be to us if the worst happens. So, no, we shouldn't take anything - except, well - there's another storage area with double what's in here, so maybe just one box?"

Dara snatched the pages from Alex's hand and flipped through them before looking up and smiling back.

"Yup, one box it is!"

The girls settled down at the desk and started to make a list of the people who they wanted to give a special gift to and then scanned the inventory sheets for what it would be. Once they had it all planned out they emptied one of the boxes of supplies onto the shelf and started to put in each gift they had chosen.

"You know this will have to be anonymous, right? There's no way we could explain where all of this came from if they asked." Dara pointed out.

"I know, and I'm ok with that. It's not us that should be getting the credit anyway. This is all from Mrs. Moore, so one day when she gets home we'll tell her what we took and if she wants, she can tell everyone. All I care about is giving our loved ones a little bit of old world happiness. Besides, it's Christmas so we'll just say it was from Santa Claus!"

Dara paused with a box of markers and a colouring book in her hand.

"Do you know how grateful I am to be able to give these to my little brother? Just this small little gift from Santa will make Christmas for him."

Alex nodded in agreement. "And a chocolate bar."

Dara's eyes lit up. "Really, I can give him one?"

Alex smiled. "Yes, but that one comes from you to him. He needs a gift from his big sister."

The girls finished filling the box and started shutting down the lanterns. When they left, Alex was careful to shuffle around in the soap flakes covering the floor of the outer room to erase their footprints and she tossed another handful down on top of the smears to cover it even more.

When they got back to the farm, they hid the box of gifts in the camper and locked it back up so no one might stumble on them before they could get them wrapped up and delivered. Alex was feeling better about things after getting away from the farm even for just a few hours. She was ready to face her parents and make a plan to get Quinn and her back on track. All of that flew out the window when the girls entered the farmhouse and saw her parents, brother and sister-in-law sitting around the table with drawn faces. Her mom jumped to her feet and raced across to them at the door, pulling Alex into her arms before pushing her back and studying her face.

"Where did you go? Did you see anyone? Did you go into anyone's house?" she asked, almost frantically.

Alex pulled away in annoyance. "Mom! Stop, we were only gone a few hours. I'm perfectly capable of looking after myself for that long, you know!"

Alex's dad intervened. "We know you are, sweetheart. It's something else. There's been an outbreak in town of some kind of flu. Three people have died from it. Dr. Mack wants everyone to self-quarantine to try and stop it from spreading. We need to know if you two went to see any of your friends."

Dara answered for them. "No, we didn't see anyone. We just went for a drive and checked on some of our caches of supplies to make sure they haven't been disturbed." She sent a quick look Alex's way to make sure she would be on board with the small lie before asking more questions. "How did you find out about this? When did it happen?"

Johnathan Andrews scrubbed at his face in relief. "Ok, that's good that you didn't have contact with anyone. Come on in and sit down and I'll tell you what we know so far." Once the girls had removed all their winter gear and settled at the table, he told them what he knew. "I took Jessie and her boys over to the Green farm to stay. They have the new long house that we were forced to build and it had a few empty rooms after some of their hands moved into town for winter. Ron had the driveway gated off and came out to meet me. He had tried to go into town this morning but the guards at the roadblock turned him back. They told him that last Sunday a man came into the community center for market day and collapsed. He was very sick and he died by the end of the day. Two days ago, people started coming down with symptoms. Every one of them had been at the market. Whatever this is, it's moving fast from person to person and as of this morning twelve more people have come down with symptoms and three more people have died from it.

"Once I told Ron that we haven't been into town or had any visitors for the last two weeks, he let us through the gate. We need to stay away from everybody until this thing burns out and Dr. Mack gives us the all clear."

Alex sat back in her chair and thought about what such an illness could do to the population of her town. With people stacked up in houses to conserve heat and resources, it could be a wildfire of contamination. A bolt of fear struck her.

"What about our friends? We need to check on the others! They might not know about this or maybe they're already sick!"

Her dad held up his hand for her to calm down. "Josh's place is fine and so is everyone living there including David and his Mom and sister. After I left the Green's I did the loop and stopped at the Mather's. They also haven't been off their property in a few weeks so Emily and Lisa are fine. The cold weather has kept us all from traveling much so that's a blessing. The last place I stopped at was The Dennison farm. Quinn, Anna and all the people they have staying on their place are clear as well. Everyone should be fine as long as we stay put and away from others. Oh, and I have a few letters for you two from your friends."

Alex sagged back in relief to know all her friends were healthy, but disappointment flooded her when she saw that there was no letter or note from Quinn. She reached up and tugged on the small ring hanging from a chain around her neck and wondered if it would ever go back on her finger or if she should just give it back.

Christmas was a very subdued version of previous years with most of the gifts Dara and Alex had chosen for their friends and family undelivered. The weather had gotten even worse with such low temperatures that the quarantine was easily enforced. Except for the mandatory chores that go into running a farm in winter, no one left the house for more than a few minutes. Tempers raised and patience frayed.

Chapter Four

Alex was miserable after rehashing everything that had gone wrong in her head. She knew she should get up and get dressed and go help her dad out in the barn but she just wanted to stay buried under the warmth of the blankets. Dara shifted in the bed beside her but made no move to get up either so she just closed her eyes again and tried not to think any more about everything that had gone wrong.

A loud round of coughing shattered the silence of the still house, causing both Alex and Dara to shoot straight up in bed. Their eyes met in panic. It was here!

Alex threw off the blankets and raced for the door but her hand hovered over the knob in fear. It only took her seconds to realize that if one of them had it, then they all did. She yanked the door open and stepped out into the icy hallway to the top of the stairs.

"Mom, MOM?" She couldn't keep the fear from her voice as she yelled down for her mom and practically dropped to her knees when her mom called back.

"It's ok, Alex! Your dad just drank some water and it went down the wrong way. He's fine. Everything is fine!"

She turned and walked slowly back to her room. Dara was sitting on the small cot with Jake in her arms and terror on her face.

"No, it's not here. Dad just swallowed some water the wrong way but I don't know how much more of this I can take."

Dara closed her eyes and let out the breath she'd been holding and then kissed Jake on the top of his head.

"Come on sleepy head, time to get up. Go on downstairs and get some breakfast. Alex and I will be right down."

Once Jake was dressed and had shuffled out of the room and headed down the stairs, Dara turned back to Alex.

"It's been almost three weeks and we haven't heard anything. It has to have run its course by now, right?"

Alex shrugged her shoulders in frustration. "I don't know, but I know I'm going to go crazy if I don't get out of here soon!"

Both girls pulled on the extra layers of clothing that would keep them from freezing even inside the house before heading downstairs to join the rest of the family. They had just taken their seats at the table for breakfast when the sound of an air horn came from the front of the property. They all jumped up and ran to the front windows to see what was going on. At the top of the driveway was an old dump truck with a plow attached to the front. The driver blew his horn again and stuck his hand out the window to wave at the house.

Johnathan pulled the front door open, letting in a draft of bitter air, and waved back at the truck before slamming it shut just as quickly.

"Peter, let's gear up and find out what he wants. You girls stay in the house please until we find out what's going on."

As much as Alex wanted to dash out there with them, she was also happy to stay inside in the semi warmth. Alberta winters had always had some harsh cold snaps but the temperatures this winter were so severe that it hurt to breathe the cold air. Once the men left the house, the girls and Jake sat down to finish the hot oatmeal breakfast. They mainly sat in silence except for the gurgling baby and Jake, who chatted about the dump truck maybe being a Transformer robot. The tension was thick with anticipation by the time the men came back into the house.

Their faces told of bad news. Johnathan dropped heavily into a chair at the table.

"Fifty-six dead and twenty-three sick. They wanted any bleach or medicines we might have left. He gave us a list of medications Dr. Mack is looking for. Alex, did you guys hold back anything from the medical supplies you brought from that vet's clinic?"

Alex looked at Dara before shaking her head. "No, we gave everything we took from there to Dr. Mack. We've got some first aid kits in the caches but I don't think there's anything in them that would fight this virus. Uh, can I see the list of medicines he gave you?"

He handed her the slip of paper while he kept telling them what they'd been told.

"They thought they had it contained for a week but then more people started coming down with it. Dr. Mack doesn't know where it's coming from, but so far it's only hit the people in town. With the quarantine and arctic temperatures, no one's been bringing food in from the farms so they're starting to run low on that too. We're going to have to put together a delivery for them. I'll do the rounds this afternoon and co-ordinate with the other farms. As long as we leave the trailer at the road block, no one should come in contact with any infected."

Alex looked up from the list. "Can Dara and I go with you? If everyone's still healthy on the other farms, then there shouldn't be any risk." When he frowned, Alex plowed ahead. "Please, Dad? We're going stir crazy here. We just want to see our friends for a few minutes!"

Peter took her side. "The guy said that all the farms on this side of town are clean. I think everybody is going stir crazy. It would be good for all of us to get away from here for a few hours. I'm sure Mom and Susan would like to visit with some of the other ladies too."

Alex almost laughed out loud when her Mom jumped to her feet in excitement.

"Yes! I mean, it would do us all some good to see other people for a change. As long as there's no risk, then we should all go."

With her mom's agreement, they all decided to go and Alex and Dara slipped back upstairs. Once they were in their room with the door closed, Alex went to her closet and pulled an old shoe box from the top shelf. Inside was handwritten copies of the medical supplies inventory at Mrs.

Moore's house. She went down the list looking for what Dr. Mack wanted but only found one match and unfortunately it was one of the medications that didn't have a huge stock. She showed it to Dara who frowned.

"I know this is really selfish but should we give it to them? There's not a lot of it and what happens if one of us or our friends get hit? It would be used up in town."

Alex's first thought at her friend's words was outrage but then she thought of all her family dying with no medicine because they had given it all away. She dropped her head in her hands in defeat. How were they supposed to make such a decision? If they didn't give it to the town and all their friends and family stayed healthy then they could be responsible for people dying but if they did give it away and their people did get sick, it would be their fault if they died. She moaned into her hands before lifting her head with an agonized expression.

"I don't know what to do!"

Dara pulled her friend into a hug. "Neither do I. Let's just take today and think about it. We'll go see the rest of the gang and maybe it will be clearer by the end of the day."

Alex nodded sadly. She was excited to get away from the farm and see her friends, but this decision would be one of the biggest of her life and it weighed very heavily on her shoulders.

Chapter Five

With the plow having cleared part of the road for them, they decided to drive the short distances between farms. The fierce cold would have been hard on all of them and the horses if they had driven over in the wagon. It was a tight fit with all six adults but they squeezed in and had Jake and the baby sit on the adult's laps.

"Wooooo Hooooo! There's MY girl!" Josh bellowed as he stomped across the snow-packed yard towards Alex and Dara when they piled out of the truck. He scooped Dara up and swung her around all while planting a huge kiss on her. When he finally let her down he moved in on Alex.

"Come here, Red. I know how jealous you get but don't worry, there's enough of me to go around!"

Alex was laughing too hard to successfully dodge his grab and ended up in her own bear hug with a smacking kiss on top of her toque covered head. She felt twenty times lighter by the time he dropped her back on her feet. She had missed him and the others so much!

"Man, am I glad to see you two. I've been feeling slightly caged here for the past few months. We really need to get everyone together, it's been way too long." Josh said.

Dara wrapped an arm around his waist and leaned into him. "No kidding. Some boyfriend you turned out to be! I've seen you like three times since the beginning of September. This weather is turning all our homes into jails."

Alex agreed. "Yeah, it's been pretty tough not being able to see everyone but it's also probably the reason none of us have gotten sick. As hard as it's been, we've been incredibly lucky too."

Josh's face turned serious. "Yeah, about that, we need to talk. Let's head over to the barn. I've got the genny running for us so the heaters are blowing. I figured the parentals could use some time away from us as much as the other way around!"

The girls followed Josh to the barn and slipped inside, grateful for the warm air that met them at the door. As soon as Josh shut the door behind them Alex and Dara started to pull their wool hats and mitts off. It was such a treat to feel the warm air against their skin but it was overshadowed by the sweet sound of familiar laughter. Alex's eyes grew wide and then she was off, racing down between the stalls to the tack room. She just stood in the doorway with the biggest grin spread across her face until she couldn't take it anymore.

"EM!!!"

Emily Mather's blond hair whipped around when she spun at the call of her nickname and she almost knocked Alex off her feet when she bolted into her.

"Oh my God, Alex! What are you doing here? I can't believe Josh didn't tell us you were coming. OH! I didn't bring your Christmas present. I've been dying to give it to you! How are you? What have you been doing? What…"

Emily's questions were stopped short by Alex pulling her into another hug. She felt tears fill her eyes as happiness flooded her heart at having her best friend with her again.

"Hey, I'm all for a lovefest, but maybe you guys could include the rest of us? Also, I didn't know any of you were coming or I would have hired a DJ for the party!" Josh joked.

Alex was beaming when she finally let go of Emily and took a good look around the rest of the room. Lisa and David were here as well. After hugs were given all around, Alex couldn't help but be slightly disappointed by their missing friend. She met Josh's eyes across the room and he read her mind with a shake of his head.

"I'm sorry, Alex. He's still checked out."

She gave him a tight smile and looked away. As sad as she was about Quinn's lack of interest in her and their friends, she was also very angry at him. The loss of his Grandfather was heartbreaking, but cutting everyone who cared about him from his life was stupid.

The group enjoyed catching up on what they had all been doing for the last few months, which mainly consisted of a whole lot of nothing as the weather and then quarantine had left all of them stuck at home, but the main topic of conversation was what was happening in town.

Emily voiced what they were all feeling. "I just wish we knew what was happening or we could at least help in some way! I feel so helpless. We don't even know who's died or who's sick!"

Josh nodded. "Dad talked to Don Carver at the road block this morning after the dump truck came through and plowed the road. We took a load of pork in when the driver said they were running low on meat. Dad wouldn't let me get out of the truck, but he filled me on what Don told him."

He looked around at his friend's faces and swallowed hard. "Almost sixty dead and many still sick. All the meds they had are gone but most of what they had in stock didn't really help anyway. Don said that they made contact with the military in Red Deer, but they aren't able or don't want to help us out with anything. Apparently, they have too many people in their camps as it is and not enough supplies. What they do have for meds they plan on holding tight to in case they get hit with the virus too, so we're on our own."

Alex and Dara's eyes met. They had a very similar dilemma with the small amount of medicine in Mrs. Moore's stockpile. They both looked away in frustration. How could they condemn the military for withholding the drugs when they were doing the exact same thing?

Josh interrupted their thoughts. "I'm sick of just sitting around here doing nothing! I want to help in some way. I don't know, maybe go find medicine or something!"

Alex looked around at the nodding, frustrated faces of her friends. They were all sick of being caged in but there wasn't any choice.

"I'm just as frustrated as the rest of you. If it was any other season I'd say let's go but this weather would kill us if we tried. The only reason we're even seeing each other today is because that plow opened up our road and we could drive. The temperature is too extreme to even think about taking the snowmobiles for more than a few miles." She shook her head, "At least we can see each other a little more now. With the road open and all of us healthy, our parents should be more open to letting us move around a bit. Let's plan on meeting at my place in a few days. Maybe we'll know more about what's happening in town after our families make a food delivery to the roadblock." Alex looked at Josh with a silent plea for him to get Quinn to come. As usual, he knew exactly what she wanted and gave a nod.

They spent the next hour catching up with each other and they were all disappointed when their parents called for them to head home. Alex's parents decided not to visit anyone else that day, she was sad and relieved all at the same time. On the one hand, she desperately wanted to mend things with Quinn, but on the other, she was terrified that he would dismiss her again, firmly closing the door on any chance they had at a future together.

Everyone in Alex's house was in a better frame of mind after getting out and socializing for a few hours but it only lasted for a couple days. There was nothing new from town when her dad dropped off supplies. It was the second day that the news he brought back sent them all into depression with a feeling of helplessness.

Her father's face was drawn and tired as he told them what he had learned. "It's worse. They had six more deaths in the last day and eight more have come down with symptoms. Dr. Mack is overwhelmed with the patients he already has at the community center so what's left of the council has decided to enforce a house by house quarantine. No one is allowed to leave their homes and move about town and anyone who comes down sick will have to stay where they are." His eyes welled up with misery. "That pretty much sentences anyone else in that house to getting the virus too. It's extreme but they hope it will keep it contained and it'll burn out this way." He rubbed at his weary face before continuing, "They can't even bury the bodies because the ground is so frozen and the remains are too dangerous to store until spring. Apparently, they've had to burn all the bodies. I understand that, but it's tragic that there can't even be funerals for the families. There will have to be a memorial service for all of them once this is over."

Alex felt sick to her stomach with grief and frustration. All she could think was there would be no memorial if no one survived the virus. Her eyes met Dara's and she saw the same emotions there as well. After everything that the town had been through and all the fighting they had done to free them, it was unbelievable that this was how it would end. She wanted to scream and rage at the world and the idiots that had caused the world to be in this state. The impotent frustration that boiled inside of her had her bolting from the kitchen.

Dara joined her in the mud room without a word as they both geared up in heavy winter outerwear. The bitter air was a slap to their faces as they left the house and headed towards the RV. Alex raised a hand to her wool-covered head and tried to rub away the headache she woke up with this morning. Her first breath of the cold air had amplified it, sending a sharp spike of pain to her temples.

The girls entered the RV and both held their breath as the engine stuttered a few times before finally catching. The cold was wearing everything down. They took their seats at the small dinette table and waited for the furnace to gradually warm up the air.

Dara shook her head with a frown before asking, "What are we going to do next winter? I mean, if we even make it through this one! The gas and propane will only last so long and then we will be totally dependent on wood for heat." When Alex just gave her a hopeless shrug, she changed the subject. "I wish we could do something to help. I feel like a monster for not handing over the small amount of medicine at Mrs. Moore's."

Alex dropped her aching head into her mitten-covered hands and groaned. "I don't think I can handle this anymore. I just want to scream in frustration. We're trapped every way I turn. It's too cold to go anywhere and search for more medicine and if we give them the little we have, what happens if one of us gets sick? There's no right answer here and I just don't want that choice on my shoulders!" She let out a deep sign and lifted her head to meet Dara's gaze. "I think we should give the meds to my parents and let them decide."

Dara frowned and bit her lip in thought before slowly nodding her head. She was about to respond when they heard the sound of engines coming closer. As one, they leaned towards the small frosted window at the end of the table and started scraping the frost from the glass to see who had come.

A grin split Dara's face as she leaned back from the window. "It's my goof boy and it looks like he brought your...err, Quinn." She finished with a wince.

Alex slid away from the window with an uncertain expression. Seeing Quinn had her heart soaring and then falling all at once. She was slightly disgusted with herself when the sight of two more snowmobiles carrying the rest of their friends filled her with relief because it meant there would be a buffer between her and Quinn.

A blast of arctic air blew through the camper as everyone climbed in and found places to sit or lean. A quick glance in Quinn's direction showed Alex his unreadable blank expression so she quickly looked away and sent smiles to the rest of her friends as they pulled off hats, gloves and scarves. Once everyone was settled, Josh launched into the latest news.

"First off, can someone please explain why we left sunny California and rushed back here to where the air literally breaks our faces? I mean, come on! This is getting ridiculous even for Alberta." He looked at all his friend's faces and let out a deep sigh before continuing. "I'm sure you've all heard what our dads learned at the roadblock today but something else has come up." He paused with a grim look before swallowing hard. "The virus has made it out of the town's borders. It sounds like a few people bolted when Dr. Mack and the council announced the quarantine of all houses. I guess they thought they could get out before they caught it but it was too late and now they've spread it to one of the farms."

Gasps and shocked expressions filled every face in the group.

"Who's farm?" Alex whispered as if saying it quietly could protect them.

Josh's expression was filled with fury before it crumpled into anguish. "The Curry's."

Alex sat back in her seat like he had punched her. The Curry farm was one of the largest farms on the south side of town and they had taken in twenty-five people from town as well as their own six. Alex had babysat their four children regularly before the lights went out. She also knew that there were at least ten other children staying on the farm with their families. The tears flowed hot like lava down her cold cheeks as her eyes flew to Dara. How could they even think about holding back the medicine from those kids?

Quinn's angry declaration interrupted her thoughts. "No one is coming onto my property! We've set up rotating guards and all of you should too!" His eyes were hard and his mouth a firm line.

Alex had never seen this side of Quinn before and she didn't know what to say. She was saved from having to respond when David jumped to his feet in anger.

"So what? You're just going to shoot anyone who comes to you for help? What is wrong with you, Quinn? What happened to turn you into this, this...jerk?"

Quinn looked at him with contempt. "Please, give me a break David! It's no different than them bringing a loaded weapon and pointing it at my family. I will do whatever it takes to protect the people I'm responsible for but it's no surprise that you wouldn't. Ever since this started you've sat back and looked down on us while all the rest of us did the dirty work to keep you and your family safe. Why change now?"

Alex surged to her feet. "Quinn! That's enough! Instead of attacking your friends, how about you help us figure out a way to fix this?"

She caught the briefest flash of sadness in his eyes when he turned to her but it quickly disappeared when he responded.

"There is no way to fix it without medicine and no one can get out to scavenge for medicine with the temperature being so low. Just coming here across the field risks frostbite! I would love to say let's go to the city and hit a hospital but we'd be dead before we made it ten miles from town! So tell me - how do you think we can fix this, Alex?"

Alex gritted her teeth against the pain in her head before bringing her hands up and rubbing at her temples in frustration.

"Arrrrr, I don't know but there's got to be something other than letting everyone die or shooting anyone who comes near us! I just can't think with this headache."

Everyone started talking and arguing at once so Alex closed her eyes and willed her headache to go away. She felt someone rubbing her back and for a brief moment she thought Quinn was back, but when she opened her eyes it was Josh standing beside her squinting at her in concern.

"I'm with you, Red. I woke up with a pounder myself. I'd roll someone for an extra strength Advil right about now!"

Alex winced in agreement but then her eyes flew wide in understanding. It took Josh a half a beat to understand as well and then his eyes flew wide too. Alex turned to the rest of the group and yelled them into quiet.

"Josh and I both have headaches! We have to go, RIGHT NOW!"

David, Emily, Dara and Lisa either leaned away or stepped back with fear on their faces but Quinn stepped towards them when understanding filled his face. "Are you sure?"

Josh's face split into his trademark grin. "Like clockwork, Buddy!"

Quinn nodded once and turned to the others. "We need a map!"

Chapter Six

Dara scanned their faces in confusion. "What's going on? Are you guys…sick?"

Josh let out a hoot and pulled her into a hug. "No way, babe! We have headaches! Alex and I always get wicked pounders the day before a chinook rolls in. You seriously could use us to forecast every chinook each winter. The weather's about to shift and the warm winds are gonna be blowing in the next twelve hours, so if we're going to make a run for medicine, we'll need to leave within the next twenty-four hours. I'm not sure how many days we'll get, but a normal chinook can last from one day to a week."

Quinn had pushed through the others to retrieve the maps from the glove box of the motorhome while Josh explained. He tossed them on the table and started to sort through them.

David threw up his hands in exasperation. "You can't seriously be thinking of going out there based on a couple of headaches!" When they just ignored him, he sighed dramatically. "Fine, let's say you're right and a chinook is about to hit, why does it have to be us? This isn't like before when we didn't have a choice about putting ourselves in danger. There are adults that can go and get the medicine! Why do you have to be the heroes again?"

Josh shot David a look of annoyance but it was Emily that responded. "David, we started being adults the day the lights when out. Of all the people in the town, the eight of us have the most experience out there on the road. Most of the adults you refer to haven't even left this small area since that day."

Josh interrupted Emily by leaning over her shoulder and wiggling his eyebrows. "Also, it's fuuuuuuun!"

David shook his head at him with a look of disbelief. "FUN? You call risking our lives and running around getting shot at and shooting people fun? Forget it! I'm out. I have a mom and sister to watch over. You guys are idiots!"

Emily stared at his retreating back as he spun and walked up to the front of the RV and settled into a seat to wait for his ride back to Josh's farm. David had changed so much since this all began. She understood some of his reasoning and his attitude, but she found herself not caring as much about him as she once had. Lisa stepped into her line of sight, breaking into her thoughts.

"Well, I'm in. The only people I have left in this world are you guys, so where you go, I go."

"Alright, alright, alright! The Maple Leaf Mafia rides again!" Josh enthused before swinging around to look at the map that Quinn had spread over the table and asked, "What's the plan?"

Quinn's eyes lifted from the map and briefly met Alex's before quickly moving to Josh. He let out a deep sigh. "Listen, as much as I disagree with David's attitude, he's right in one aspect. I also have people I need to watch over. I don't think I can go with you on this."

Josh glanced at Alex and then down to the map. The tightness in his jaw and mouth were the only signs that Quinn's words had affected him. His voice was a flat neutral when he responded.

"Yeah, sure man. We get it." He angled his back away from Quinn and said dismissively, "Why don't you give David a lift back to my place?" and turned his attention to Alex.

"I think we should hit Red Deer first. Cooper is still there with the military. Maybe he can give us some inside help. If we can get the meds there it'll save us from having to go all the way to Calgary."

Alex was looking over Josh's bent head straight into Quinn's eyes. She saw the flash of anger in them at Josh's words but they quickly turned blank so she just started nodding her head. "Yeah, Cooper's exactly who we need. He's always been there for us."

The sadness in her heart hardened when Quinn just gave a sharp nod before turning and barking a "Let's go" to David as he climbed down the steps and left.

There was tense silence in the camper until the sound of Quinn's snowmobile faded away. Dara looked around at Alex, Emily and Lisa's faces before addressing Josh.

"Well, looks like you're getting that harem you always wanted."

It was a testament to how upset he was that her statement didn't bring a grin to his face but just a brief uplift of his lips.

"Yeah, that's me, total ladies man. Besides, let's be honest, you four badasses could probably go get this done with your eyes closed." He leaned over and planted a kiss on Dara's forehead. "Are you sure you want to come on this run? What about Jake?"

She gave a quick nod. "It's because of Jake that I want to go." She looked at Alex with a question and received a nod of agreement. "There's something you guys should know. Alex and I have a small amount of the medicine that Dr. Mack says fights this virus. It's not very much so we decided to hold it back in case some of our group got sick. That decision's been killing us!"

Emily and Lisa frowned but then started nodding. Emily reached out a hand and squeezed Alex's shoulder.

"What a crappy thing to have to decide. I'm sorry you guys had to make that decision but I think you were right."

Lisa threw an arm around Dara. "It's a terrible world we live in right now. It forces us to make decisions that we would never have considered a half a year ago. Thankfully, we're going to get a chance to try and save everybody. Focus on that."

Alex brushed away the tears that had welled up in her eyes. "We have six courses of medicine. I think we should hold back two and give four to the Curry's. It's not enough but it might save some of the kids until we can get back with enough for everyone."

They nodded in agreement, causing Alex to feel the huge weight on her shoulders to lessen. She blew out a breath and looked down at the map before continuing. "Ok, it's around eighty kilometres to Red Deer or two hundred and twenty to Calgary. Let's say we have to go into Calgary so we'll need at least enough gas for say, four hundred and sixty kilometres round trip with a buffer. We need to do some math and figure out how much we need to take with us. There's five of us so we'll need to take three sleds with at least one trailer, maybe two with some trade goods. Josh, you know your vehicles, so what's the magic number?"

Josh started drawing numbers in the air with a finger as he walked them through the math.

"Alright, pay attention class! Each sled can go anywhere from a hundred to a hundred and twenty kilometres on one tank with a nice steady ride. Each tank takes forty litres to fill so if we leave here with a full tank in all three sleds, we'll need to carry another four full tanks worth of fuel with us to make it round trip." He raised his eyebrows in thought before shaking his head. "Not doable! That's too much gas to haul. Even bringing enough for a one-way trip is a lot, so I say we take enough with us to get to Calgary and then plan to siphon the rest as we go. The city had over a million people before lights out. There's going to be plenty of cars to drain when we get there. It's been nine months since the day, so the gas should be good for a while yet sealed up in tanks, but it's going to start going bad in the not so far future without stabilizers added to it. That's going to be a sucky day! No lights, no heat *and* no wheels? I'm going to have to find me a donkey to ride with a heated saddle!"

Alex rolled her eyes and laughed for what felt like the first time all day. Lisa shook her head with a smile but then killed the mood with a question. "What do you think your parents are going to say about this trip? They've been keeping us all on a pretty short leash since we got back."

With frowns all around the table, it was Emily that shrugged her shoulders and answered.

"Listen, they love us and want to protect us, but this is something I'm deciding for myself. Like I said, I'm not a kid anymore and I'm capable of taking care of myself. And really, I'm kinda sick and tired of being trapped on one small piece of land. I'm going. Lisa, you're living with us but you don't have parents to answer to so the choice is yours to make." She turned to the other three and raised her eyebrows in question.

Dara turned to Josh,

"I want to go too but I can't just leave Jake here for Alex's parents to watch over."

Josh waved her concern away. "My parents love Jake. I'll take him back to my place today and he can stay there. Besides, he's the only kid here now, at least at my place there are other kids for him to hang out with. As for permission to go? Well, I like that old saying about asking forgiveness is sometimes easier than asking for permission! I plan on leaving a note for them and then sneaking out at dawn."

Alex nodded. "Yeah, I'm with you on that. The responsible "adult" thing to do would be to tell them what we have planned, but I just don't have it in me to fight with them about this. I do think that when we get home from this run we need to sit down with them and have a talk about the restrictions they've put on us and the reality of us being old enough and mature enough to make our own decisions." Emily and Josh's faces echoed her determination so she nodded and changed the subject.

"OK, we need to get moving. Josh, you and Dara should round up Jake and then head out. We'll tell my parents that we are going over to your place for a visit and then me and the girls will make a run out to some of our caches to load up supplies. I'll need to get the sled trailer from your place anyway. If everything goes to plan and the temperature starts to rise, we'll all meet at the turnoff to town at dawn."

Everyone stood up to leave when Josh held up his hand. "Two things. One, bring the big guns and a handgun for each of us with lots of ammo. If we have to go all the way to Calgary, there's no telling what we might run into. Two, I'm sorry about Quinn, Alex. I don't even know what to say any more about him."

Alex's lips thinned into a hard line and she shook her head. "There's nothing to say. He's changed. Whatever decisions he's making are his to make. I need to focus on doing something to help our town, not my love life."

As far as Alex was concerned, that future was gone.

Chapter Seven

The four girls spent a busy day preparing for the next dawn's departure. They loaded the two sled trailers with jerry cans of gas and supplies from the caches they had set up back in the summer after the town had been freed. All the teens had agreed back then that the new world was too unpredictable to have all their supplies in one place. They wanted to ensure that they would have access to what they needed if something forced them from their homes again. With all the hard work they had put in that summer on the farms, they had all made time when their parents allowed them to go scavenge for more valuable goods.

Each of the three caches had a good supply of stored fuel, first-aid kits and food. They all knew just how hard these things would be to come by in the future so they used what they had accumulated very cautiously. This trip would put a dent in it but it was for the greater good.

The girls left the packed trailers well camouflaged at the base of their old tree fort hideout. They would pick them up before they left in the morning. Once Lisa and Emily had left for home, Alex and Dara made the quick trip to Mrs. Moore's place to grab the medicine and a few other items that they thought might come in handy on the trip, like the walkie talkies. Alex's hand had hovered over the bulk-sized bottle of Advil for a moment before pulling it back, there were more important things the pain reliever could be used for than a headache. Dara nudged her aside with a shake of her head and opened the bottle, spilling ten tablets into her palm and holding them out to Alex.

"We have a possibly dangerous trip tomorrow. You and Josh both need to bring your "A" game. That's not going to happen if both of you are squinting through migraines. Take some for both of you!" When Alex still hesitated, Dara rolled her eyes. "Seriously, this stuff is important but it's not helping anybody sitting here getting ready to expire. If it'll help keep you and Josh sharp on this trip then it might BE life or death to us." She thrust the pills at Alex with a stern look. A piercing headache and Dara's words were enough to convince Alex, so she threw back two of the pills and pocketed the rest before they shut down the lanterns and headed for home.

Both the girls were cold to the bone as they finally parked the sled in the barn for the day, but Alex thought that the air had less of a bite than a few hours ago.

Alex was grateful for the hearty stew and biscuits her mom had made for supper but she struggled to get through the meal while pretending that everything was normal. She knew what kind of fallout would welcome her and Dara when they got back from the trip. She hated keeping secrets from her family but as long as they continued to treat her like a child in need of constant protection, she felt like she didn't have a choice. She tried to explain how she felt in the note she left for her parents, but it just sounded like excuses for taking off to her.

By the time the two girls crawled into bed for the night, Alex was exhausted. Thankfully the Advil had taken the edge off of her migraine, but it didn't help her sleep any better. Judging by Dara's restless movements throughout the night, they would both be tired the next day.

It was a relief when the darkness of the bedroom started to lighten and both girls threw back the covers and got dressed. They were almost completely silent as they shouldered their backpacks and crept down the hall to the stairs. Both girls avoided the third step from the top that always creaked and made it down the stairs without alerting anyone in the house. They both froze in their tracks with their feet halfway into their boots when they heard the baby start fussing. They held their breath waiting for the full-on cry but it never came, so they quickly finished dressing in the winter gear and slipped out of the house.

It wasn't until they had made it across the yard and to the barn that Alex realized her exposed face wasn't stinging from the bitter air. The temperature had risen a lot. The night before they had parked the sled at the back end of the barn so when they left this morning they would have the barn between them and the house. The two of them worked up a sweat pushing the heavy machine out of the yard and down the trail into the woods. In this new world, sound carried easily so they wanted to be as far from the house as possible before they started the machine. They were both out of breath when they finally got deep enough into the woods that they felt they could start the sled up and ride the rest of the way.

When they got to the clearing where they had left the sled trailers, Emily and Lisa were already waiting for them. The four girls stood looking at each other with serious expressions until Emily's face cracked into a grin.

"I know how bad things are in town but I can't help but feel excited about this trip. Does that make me a horrible person?"

Alex shook her head. "Well, I guess I'm horrible too then, cuz I feel almost relief that we are about to take off."

Lisa let out a deep sigh, "Thank you! I thought I was reverting back to my old selfish self. I've been secretly thrilled to get out of here with you guys!"

Dara smiled. "It's not that were being horrible or selfish. We're a team, a family and we all bonded deeply over what happened at the beginning of summer. We got used to taking charge and getting the job done together. Now we get to do it again and it feels good!"

Alex nodded. "Yes, exactly! So let's go get what our people need. Come on ladies, Josh is waiting for us."

The girls made quick work of hooking up the trailers and then headed deeper into the woods away from Alex's property. They traveled in a loop around all the teen's properties in the ever-brightening light until they finally crested a small hill and could see the turnoff to town below. Alex was in the lead and she slowed her machine when she spotted two people standing beside a snowmobile with a trailer sled attached to it down below. Her heart clenched for a second when she recognized Quinn standing with Josh. She didn't know if he was there to see them off or if he had changed his mind and was going to join them. Dara gave her waist a squeeze in encouragement as she sped back up.

When the girls pulled up to them on the road only Dara dismounted and removed her helmet. She walked over to Josh and planted a kiss on his grinning face. He swung an arm around her shoulders and turned to Alex and the two other girls.

"Hey, hey! I brought some more testosterone with me to help us save the world!"

Dara hip-bumped him. "Hmmm, that's probably a good idea. I doubt you could handle four women on your own!" She flashed a look Alex's way before addressing Quinn. "Quinn, glad you changed your mind. So what's with the extra trailer? I thought we were only going to bring two."

Quinn's expression was blank as he stared at Alex but she had kept her visor down so he couldn't see her face. He finally turned away with a sigh and answered Dara.

"The best chance we have of getting the meds we need will be if we have something the army wants. I went over to Josh's place last night and we packed the trailer with frozen beef and pork. I'm hoping it will be enough to get the trade done so we can get back here faster."

Emily flipped up her helmet visor and spoke up, "I was thinking the same thing. I have around ten dozen eggs packed in the insulated carrier we use for going to market. As long as the temperature stays this warm, they shouldn't freeze. I wish I could have brought more but I was trying to keep my parents from noticing they were gone until after we left. How did you two manage to take that much meat without getting caught?"

Josh look down at his feet and dug his boot into the snow so Quinn answered her.

"We told them. I had to let the men on my farm know what I was doing so they could manage things without me. My Gram's gave us her blessing." He looked over at Josh and a small smile tugged at the corner of his mouth. "Josh's mom flipped and his dad cried about what a brave boy he had raised. Then they helped us pack the trailer."

Emily shook her head in frustration. "I wish I could have told them but I know for a fact my dad would have stood outside my bedroom door with a shotgun to keep me from leaving. I'm sure Alex's dad would have done the same." When Alex still didn't lift her visor to respond she looked back at the boys. "Whatever, it's done now so let get going."

Dara pulled off her glove and dug into her pocket before holding her hand out to Josh. When he looked down into her palm and saw the two, extra strength Advils there, his eyes got huge and he dramatically dropped to his knees in the snow with his hand over his heart.

"My God woman, say you'll marry me, right here, right now!"

The grin on her face dimmed as she slid a quick glance over at Quinn who quickly looked away with a frown. It wasn't that long ago that he'd asked Alex that same question.

She shook her head and hauled Josh back to his feet. "Take your medicine, fool!"

Dara gave Josh another quick kiss and started to walk back over to the sled Alex was driving. He looked to her and then Quinn in question before asking, "Hey, aren't you going to ride with me?"

Dara tossed a smug look over her shoulder at him. "Nope, I'm good with Alex. Enjoy your testosterone!"

Josh sent a glower Quinn's way before waving him onto the back of his sled. He quickly downed the painkillers for his pounding headache and once Quinn was settled, climbed on to the sled and pulled out.

He led the group east under a brightening sky that highlighted the distinctive chinook cloud arch. It was a smooth ride on the flat unplowed road and it seemed to fly by once they reached the main highway that would take them all the way to Red Deer.

Halfway there, Alex couldn't help but feel like they were the only people left in this area of the province. Even though it was still very early in the day, they hadn't seen anyone out on the road or in the few homes that dotted the landscape. She figured that would change as they got closer to the city and the temperature continued to rise.

Alex hoped they had success with the military in Red Deer so they could get back home quickly and deliver the lifesaving medicine that so many people in their town needed. At the same time, with every kilometer of distance that they put between themselves and home, she felt a weight lifting off of her shoulders. The guilt at feeling that way came but she pushed it aside. She couldn't help feeling that way so there was no point in dwelling on it.

As the group came upon the exit to a lake town twenty kilometres from Red Deer, Dara squeezed Alex's waist to get her attention and pointed to the north where part of the town could be seen from the highway. Alex slowed the sled to get a better look at what she was pointing at.

There were smoke trails coming from a scattering of homes closest to the lake and groups of small, distant figures could be seen out on the ice of the lake. Alex figured they were ice fishing. Dara patted her shoulder and pointed ahead to show her that the other two sleds were pulling away from them so Alex sped back up. She was happy to know that there was life surviving out here.

The highway widened to a divided four-lane at that point, letting the group speed up even more and the last few kilometres flew by. Josh was in the lead and as they approached the last rise before the city, he slowed his sled and came to a stop right before the crest. The girls pulled in behind him and shut their machines down.

Everyone dismounted and removed their helmets so they could plan their next steps. Josh went to his trailer, unhooked the tarp and hefted out one of the jerry cans of gas while Quinn started to hike up the hill.

"We should fill all the tanks before we go any further. I doubt there will be any problems but just in case we should be ready to run if we have to. Quinn's going to check if there are any road blocks in place."

The girls worked on filling their gas tanks with their own jerry cans as they waited for Quinn to report back on what was on the other side of the rise. By the time he made it back down to them, they had all gassed up and were waiting on him.

Emily tossed him a bottle of water before asking, "What did you see?"

He shook his head then took a deep drink before capping it and tossing it back.

"Nothing there. The road's open all the way into the city. As far as I could tell, most of the city looks empty. There's a lot of smoke trails coming from the southern end so my guess is they've set up camp over there and left the rest empty." He turned away so Josh took over.

"Makes sense, there's a lot of hotels and the fairgrounds over there to house them. There's no way they have enough troops to cover the whole city. I think we should take the number two highway to circle around to the south and put us closer to where they're set up. There's lots of industrial buildings along that road. We should pick one, hide the sleds and walk in from there. That way no one will think of getting grabby for our transportation and supplies."

Alex looked at the girls, avoiding Quinn's eyes, and nodded.

"We should also leave the rifles behind and only take the handguns. Remember how they confiscated all the AK's we had handed out to the men after we freed them from the barns? No sense losing any more of them!"

Everyone agreed with the plan so they mounted back up and continued towards the city, taking the exit that looped south. As they passed many deserted oilfield service buildings and yards full of abandoned equipment, Alex wondered if her oil and natural gas rich province would ever recover enough to pump the precious resources from the ground again.

The group followed Josh's sled off the road when he made a quick turn into a parking lot that housed a huge agricultural farm machinery dealership. Connected to it was a smaller dealership that sold utility and recreation vehicles. They drove around to the back of the building where huge garage doors led into maintenance bays. When he pulled up to the doors and shut his machine down, they all did the same and climbed off.

Alex pulled her helmet and toque off and shook out her long red curls in the much warmer air before turning to Josh.

"What's up? This is way too far to walk the rest of the way?"

Josh was rummaging around in his sled's trailer before coming up with a pair of bolt cutters and grinning at her.

"Yeah, we'll park somewhere closer but I just remembered this place as we were driving up to it. Last spring, Dad and I were here to buy the new baler. While he was doing the paperwork, I wandered over to this side and took a look around. They sell all kinds of snowmobiles and UTV's. They had a bunch being worked on in the garage. Also, they have their own gas pumps so I thought it would be a good idea to try and top up our jerry cans here and look for anything useful before we went any closer. That way if we strike out and have to head south to Calgary we'll be ready to go. I don't want to miss anything we might be able to use from here if we're coming back this way after dark or if the weather turns on us."

Alex nodded and turned to Dara, Emily and Lisa. "Why don't we grab some breakfast while we wait for the guys to scavenge? I don't know about you guys but I'm starving!"

The girls agreed and started to rummage around in their own trailers for something easy to eat. None of them had been able to make travel food without their parents knowing what they were up to so it was a real treat when Josh stopped them and tossed a backpack their way.

"Mom to the rescue! She packed a couple thermoses of hot oatmeal, sandwiches and snacks for lunch."

Dara caught the bag and blew him a kiss.

"Keep it up Green and I just might say yes to that question you asked this morning!"

Josh wiggled his eyebrows at her before he turned and got to work on the bay door locks. Quinn kept his expression blank but his eyes followed Alex as she helped Dara pass out some of the food from the pack. He kept watching her until Josh let out a "whoop" and rolled up one of the doors.

Josh turned to the group and made an exaggerated bow but it turned into a pout when he saw that the girls were too busy eating to notice. Instead, he just waved Quinn into the building ahead of him.

Once the boys had disappeared into the dark garage, Emily pinned Alex with a questioning look. "Are you ok?"

Alex glanced over towards the door and let out a sigh. "Yeah, I'm half glad he came and half annoyed. On the one hand, it feels right for him to be with us but on the other, I don't really appreciate the walking on egg shells around him that everyone has to do. I wish he would just talk to me and get it over with! There's enough crap going on right now without his man drama!"

Lisa let out a snort. "Funny how he wasn't coming until Josh brought up Cooper!"

Dara let out a laugh. "Annnnnd, the triangle is back!"

Alex rolled her eyes in annoyance and started shaking her head. "NO. IT'S. NOT! The first time was bad enough. I'm not going there again!"

Dara's eyes danced with teasing amusement. "Poor Alex, torn between two men. Will she ever find her happy ever after?"

As the other girls burst into laughter, Alex narrowed her eyes and pretended to cock an imaginary shotgun. After she had pretended to shoot each one of her friends, she sent them a sweet smile and a wink. Even with everything going on with the virus and Quinn, she was just so happy to be back together with her friends.

The girls all turned to watch as Josh came back outside and scanned the lot for something. Whatever he was looking for was located in the far back corner of the lot. He let out a deep sigh and started wading through the untouched snow in that direction.

Dara raised her eyebrows in question, but the girls just shook their heads so she yelled over to him. "Hey, where are you going?"

Josh stopped and turned back towards them with a mocking scowl and put his hands on his hips.

"You know, you guys could help scavenge with us. It would speed things up. After all, we DO have places to BE and people to SAVE!"

When none of the girls answered him or moved from where they were sitting, he threw his hands in the air and turned to stomp through more snow.

Dara turned back to her friends and raised her face up to the sky with her eyes closed.

"This is the first time in months that I've been able to sit outside and not feel like something important on my body was going to freeze and fall off!" She paused for a few seconds and then got to her feet. "Well, that was nice! I guess I better go rescue him from a snowdrift he's bound to fall into."

Alex jumped to her feet. "Yup, I'll come with you to help pull him out!"

Emily and Lisa rose as well and with smirks on their faces headed towards the open garage door where they could hear Quinn banging around. Emily looked back at Alex over her shoulder and hissed "Chicken!" with a smile.

Alex just nodded in agreement and followed after Dara.

Chapter Eight

"What exactly do you think we need from inside here, Josh?" Dara asked with impatience from down on her knees, where she and Alex were scooping snow with their gloved hands to clear the door of a metal shipping container.

He looked down from where he was trying to use the bolt cutters on multiple locks and grinned. "According to these shipping manifests I found, there are a bunch of Sno-Cobra ski and track attachments in here. They replace the wheels on ATV's and UTV's so they work like snowmobiles. If they're in there then it's a great find. It'll give us more vehicles to use in all this snow once we mount them on our machines back home!"

Alex leaned back on her heels and looked up at him. "Ok, that is a great find, but do we really have time to be doing this right now?"

Josh strained to snap through the final lock on the door before answering her. "We left at dawn so I'm guessing it's no later than eight, eight-thirty, right now. We have the whole day to get the meds and get home but by the time we do all that it might be too late in the day to stop here again and get this stuff. We have to make this trip count in every way possible, so yes, I think doing it now is necessary."

Alex nodded. "Yes, I agree that getting more resources for home is a good thing, but what if we can't get the meds from the military? We'll have to head to Calgary and search the hospitals there. That's going to take a lot of time."

Josh looked to Dara and then back to Alex with a resigned frown. "Listen, Red. If we have to go all the way to Calgary for the meds, we won't be making it home today." Alex started to interrupt so Josh held up his hand in a hold on gesture before continuing. "I know we figured we could do it in a day when we planned it out but let's be realistic here. If we leave Red Deer by eleven or noon to head south, it'll take at least three hours to get to Calgary. That's if nothing goes sideways. Then, say another three or four hours in the city if we get lucky and find what we need at the first hospital we go to.

"Don't forget just how spread out everything is in that city! I read once that the land mass of that city is over eight hundred square kilometres. Dad told me last night that there are five major hospitals and only two of them are close together. The other three are spread out in the different quadrants. It could take us a whole day of searching if we have to go to each of them. But again, let's say we get lucky and hit the right one first off. By the time we get in and then out of that city it will be sometime around four or five and that's when it gets dark now. Do you want to try and drive three or four hours in the dark? The cloud arch won't let even the moonlight through." He paused and shook his head. "Sorry Alex, it would be too dangerous. We would have to find somewhere to camp out for the night. SO, think positive and hope we can get the meds from the military here!"

Alex's shoulders slumped but she nodded so he turned to disengage the last sheared lock on the door and gave a tug to try and open it. The one door swung out about four inches before it stopped against the snow so they all got back to shoveling the deep white stuff out of the way. It only took the three of them five more minutes to clear enough of a path to swing both the doors open enough for them to enter.

Whoever worked at the dealership had already removed quite a bit from it, but there were still boxes on pallets so they hoped that the parts they were looking for would still be inside. The light was dim but Josh had brought a working flashlight that he used to scan the part numbers on the side of the boxes as the girls tore off plastic wrap from some of the stacks. Josh leaned back from the third pallet he had checked and shook his head before going straight to the back of the container. He mumbled as he passed them.

"It's always the last one you check, so start at the last one."

The girls ignored him as they moved on to the next pallet. As they pulled the plastic wrap away from the boxes they both saw the words SNOCOBRA printed on the boxes. Dara called out, "Found them!" just as Josh let out a little kid squeal.

Alex and Dara moved towards the back of the container to see what had Josh so interested and found him lovingly running his hands over a shiny red UTV. He turned and gave them a sad look like someone had just stolen his puppy.

Dara gave him a pitying look. "That's a really nice paperweight you got there. Maybe you could push it home and use it as a flower box!"

Josh scowled at her. "You're so mean! This right here is a fully loaded tricked out Ranger crew XP 1000. Look, it even has the doors, windshield and soft top!" He turned back to it and patted the roof before muttering, "I really wanted one of these."

Dara shook her head at him as Alex just smirked in amusement.

"Well, I really wanted the latest iPhone but that's never going to happen now so let's get the boxes you wanted and get going!"

Josh ignored her, opened the door to the utility vehicle and climbed in behind the steering wheel.

The girls turned away and started to walk back towards the boxes they had found when the sound of the engine starting up had them both whirling around in complete shock.

Josh was pounding on the steering wheel and whooping with the biggest grin on his face.

Alex and Dara waved at him to shut the machine down. The noise of the engine was deafening in the enclosed metal unit. As soon as he turned the key to off and they could hear again, Dara and Alex started firing questions at him.

"How did you do that?"

"How is that possible? That thing should be just as dead as everything else!"

Josh just started laughing and threw up his hands.

"Whoa, whoa, ladies! What can I say? It must be my magic touch!"

Dara just laughed but Alex asked,

"Seriously, Josh, how is that still working?"

Josh looked over the dashboard and then up at the ceiling before answering.

"I'm not a hundred percent positive but I think it being inside surrounded by metal protected it from the EMP somehow. It's up on a pallet so maybe the pulse didn't get it?" He shook his head and grinned with glee. "Don't care! I got me a new toy!"

Dara just nodded in amusement and glanced back at the opening of the container before waving him out of the vehicle.

"Well, yay for you! Now get over here and start helping us clear a path so you can drive that thing out of here. Time's ticking away buddy and we have stuff to do!"

The three of them worked together to move boxes out of the way and stand the wooden pallets up against the walls of the container until there was enough room for Josh to drive the UTV out into the sun and snow. They loaded the cargo bed with the Sno-Cobra parts they would need and then drove back over to the garage. They only had to shovel it out three times when it got stuck in the deeper snow.

Quinn, Lisa and Emily were each carrying a jerry can of gas when they came out of the garage to meet them. The girl's expressions were filled with surprise but Quinn cracked a rare smile and just shook his head. It had been so long since Alex had seen him smile that her heart lurched painfully in her chest at the reminder of why she loved him.

He dropped his gas can in the snow and walked around the new machine to get a good look at it before turning to Josh and giving him a hi-five.

"Man, only you would find the only working toy that you've always wanted in the apocalypse!"

Josh puffed out his chest and gave an exaggerated bow. "You may call me King of the Scavengers!"

Quinn huffed out a laugh. "It's great but those wheels aren't going to make it home in all of the snow. We'll have to stash it somewhere safe and come back for it after the melt."

Josh held up a finger. "Ah, ah, ah, au contraire! Observe the other scavenged items in the cargo bed. I give you the Sno-Cobra ski and track system. Designed to turn any utility vehicle into a snowmobile! I'm gonna drive this baby into the garage and swap out the wheels in no time. Today, we ride in style!"

Quinn nodded slowly in appreciation and then looked down at the old watch on his wrist.

"Alright, let's get it done and get going. It's already nine thirty and it'll take at least an hour to mount the parts."

Josh snorted. "Pfff, it's not going to take me that long, but yeah, let's get on it. How did you guys make out for gas?"

Lisa spoke up. "We siphoned enough to top off the tanks and refill our cans so we're good to go." She turned to the other girls. "While these two play mechanic, why don't we go into the office and showroom area and see if there's anything worth taking."

Josh nodded and jumped back into the UTV. He fired it up with another grin and drove it into the garage bay where all the tools he would need were waiting for him. The girls headed deeper into the building.

The first room they came to was the staff lunch room. It had already been thoroughly searched and the glass door to the vending machine had been smashed open.

It didn't take them very long to clear the building. It was clear that someone else had been through it before them so they settled into a small seating area with leather love seats in the front lobby and waited for the boys to finish up in the garage. They chatted at first but the combination of soft couches and little sleep the night before had each girl nodding off.

Forty-five minutes later, Josh and Quinn stood looking down at the sleeping girls with amused expressions. Josh went over to Dara and planted a kiss on top of her head to wake her. Quinn went to Alex and without thinking gently tugged on one of her red curls. That simple action brought back the memories of his grandfather doing that exact action so many times. The flood of pain was immediate and brought a harsh scowl to his face so that's what Alex saw when she opened her eyes. Her reaction was to bat his hand away and heave herself to her feet.

She turned her back to him so she missed seeing the sadness that flashed across his face and asked Josh, "Are we ready to go?"

Josh looked past her at Quinn and let out a sigh before looking back at her and giving her a nod.

"Let's hit it."

Chapter Nine

Everyone's legs were aching from walking through the deep snow by the time the manned barricade came into sight. They had stashed their machines, including the new UTV, in two different places. Half behind a partially burned out office building and the other half behind another building down the road. Both stashes were covered by a tarp with snow piled on top. If someone were to stumble upon them, they would hopefully only lose half of their machines and supplies. They had also left their assault rifles behind and only carried concealed handguns.

Walking through the deep drifts was slow going, but it would have been worse if there hadn't been some old ruts made by a vehicle. The ruts weren't fresh but they had packed down some of the snow giving the group an easier trail to follow.

When they reached the barricade that consisted of two yellow school buses fronted with concrete barriers, they were all breathing hard and sweating in their snow gear. The temperature continued to climb from the bone-numbing cold they had grown used to.

Four bored looking soldiers greeted them with half raised rifles. One of them stepped forward and nodded back the way the group had come from.

"No room in the Inn, folks! We aren't accepting any new refugees until spring. Come back then and there'll be a place for you if you're willing to help with the crop planting."

Josh dropped his pack to the snow and shook his head with a smile.

"Uh, yeah, thanks for the offer but we'll be planting our own crops then. We aren't here as refugees. One of our friends joined up with you guys after your medics patched him up. We were hoping to check up on him and maybe do some trades while we were here."

The three other soldiers started smirking as the one who had spoken started shaking his head before Josh had even finished speaking.

"Do you know how many citizens we have packed into the hotels and apartments in this area? There's no way you'll find one guy in that mess! Sorry pal, but what do have to trade? We can do that here."

Josh cocked his head to the side and gave him a condescending look. He knew that any "trade" with these guys would be more like confiscate than anything else.

"Sorry, I wasn't clear on that. Our friend enlisted with your outfit. So he should be fairly easy to find, right?"

The soldier's eyebrows shot up. "Your guy is one of us, military?" When Josh nodded and gave Cooper's name, one of the other soldiers stepped forward.

"Hey, I know Coop. He's got a rack in my barracks. He's a good grunt. If these are his people, it'll make his day."

The first soldier frowned and then shook his head again. "No, we aren't supposed to let any more in. These guys could just get lost in the crowd and then we've got six more mouths to feed. Sorry, man, orders are orders."

Alex pulled out the paper bag with what was left of the lunch Josh's mom had packed for them and stepped forward. She held it up and asked, "Is food tight for the people here?"

When one of the soldiers snorted and said, "Food? More like slop!" Alex nodded and tossed him the bag. He let his rifle swing down to catch it and looked warily at her before opening the bag. His eyes grew wide before he stuck his nose into the bag and took a deep smell. When his head came up his eyes were filled with awe.

"Holy, Mary, Mother of Tim Horton's!" When he passed the bag to the soldier who was refusing them entry Alex spoke.

"That's just a snack for the trip. Do you really think we would trade everything that comes with that for your "slop"? We just want to check on our friend and get home before the temperature drops again." When the soldier reluctantly tried to hand the bag back to her, she shook her head. "Keep it. Call it a gift, toll or admission, whatever. Just send us to the right place to find our friend and we'll pay again in a few hours when we leave."

The soldier gave her a hard look. "Are you trying to bribe me?"

Alex gave him her sweetest smile and batted her eyelashes at him. "Why yes, yes I am!"

He stared her down for a few more seconds before the corner of his mouth twitched like he was fighting a smile. He finally gave up and shrugged.

"Fresh baked muffins and a pretty redhead fake flirting with me? Yeah, that's about all it takes these days." He turned to one of the other soldiers and addressed him. "Fire up the radio and find out where their grunt is right now then come eat your damn muffin! BUT...I got dibs on the crab apples." He turned back to Alex. "My little girls get those tonight."

As soon as the group got directions to Cooper's location they were let through the roadblock. It was much easier going from there on because a path had been plowed in the snow down the middle of the road. They didn't see anyone else on the empty street until they rounded a bend and the road opened up to a commercial area. The group stopped in their tracks at the sight of more people than any of them had seen since last spring in California. There were hundreds of people out on the streets moving around. Alex figured with the warming temperatures that this was the first time most of the people would have been able to spend any time outdoors since the first snow.

As they started up again and got closer, she got a better look at some of the people milling around and was saddened by their condition. Almost all of them had gaunt, grey faces like they were near to starving with their coats practically hanging off of their thin frames. Alex didn't see a single person that look healthy or well fed and it reminded her to be thankful for all that she and her friends had that these people didn't.

She saw one group of children that were sitting around a tired looking woman who was reading to them from a school textbook. None of the children were smiling or seemed very interested and Alex couldn't help but think of the contrast between this year's first chinook and previous years. Winters in Alberta have traditionally been very cold but there were always chinooks to break it up. In years past, the first chinook of the season would have children exploding outside to run and play in the snow without fear of frostbite. These kids looked like they didn't have the energy to learn, let alone play. She had to look away from their small listless faces. After they passed the group, she just put her head down and followed behind Josh and Dara who were in the lead.

No one spoke as they wound their way through the throngs of people until Josh came to a stop and pointed at a large warehouse in a row of them across the street.

"I think this is the place."

The front of the building was devoid of anyone and it looked just as deserted as all the other buildings, but the sound of metal crashing could be heard from around the back so the group skirted around to see if they could find anyone to direct them to Cooper.

When they rounded the corner of the building they saw rows of dumpsters piled high with scrap metal. People were carrying more out of big bay doors and dumping their loads into the bins. Spying a man in uniform holding a clipboard, Josh headed in his direction with the others following close behind.

When they got a few feet from him, he looked up and frowned at them.

"What are you doing? Break isn't for another hour. Get back to work!"

Josh's face split into a grin in response to this guy thinking they worked here and he shook his head and joked,

"Nope, day off! We're just looking for a friend of ours. Is Cooper Morris around?"

The soldier took a better look at the group of teens and confusion spread across his face when he realized that these kids didn't look like most of the beaten down citizens of the city.

"Uh, yeah, stay here. I'll go get him."

Alex turned away and looked out at the rows of dumpsters to try and figure out what they were doing here. The fences between the warehouses had been pulled down so that there was a long lot running behind them and all snow had been cleared from the area. A few buildings down, she could see thousands of windows in frames stacked up and leaning against each other. Further down the lot, there was what looked like different types of lawn equipment. There were riding mowers and push mowers as well as weed whackers. The bins closest to them were filled with pieces and parts of small electronics and appliances. There was some major scavenging happening in this city to produce this much scrap. A sharp intake of breath had her turning back to her friends.

Standing in the bay door looking out at them was a soldier. His close-cropped black hair was a real change from the thick curls he used to sport but there was no mistaking the green eyes that zeroed in on her. The last time she had seen him, Cooper had been on his back with a bullet wound to his chest. He had been shot when he rushed the leader of the gang that had been holding their families hostage as slave labour. At the time, that man had been using Alex as a shield to try and escape from their retaken town.

The look in his eyes now told Alex that he still had feelings for her and it caused a pang in her heart for the pain she had caused him by choosing Quinn instead. She stepped forward to speak but Josh beat her to it.

"Coop! Man, it's good to see you on your feet." He stepped up to him and pounded him on the back.

Cooper tore his eyes from Alex and returned Josh's smile, pulling him into a one-armed man hug. Even though it was a huge surprise to see his friends, it made him incredibly happy. They had formed close bonds traveling back from California after the lights went out and he had missed all of them very much. He felt like it was the right decision to not return to Prairie Springs after he had healed up, but it didn't change the hole that was left from missing the first real friends he had in his life.

He pulled back from Josh and accepted hugs from Dara, Emily and Lisa before turning to Quinn. Something about his friend's face had changed since he had seen him last. There was a hardness there and his eyes didn't hold the usual warmth that Cooper remembered. He hoped Quinn wasn't holding a grudge over his feelings for Alex. After all, she had chosen Quinn in the end.

Cooper held out his hand to Quinn. There was a brief hesitation but then the other boy's face softened slightly and he reached back and shook Cooper's hand.

"Cooper, it's good to see you."

Cooper nodded. "Yeah, nice to see you guys without bullets flying our way." He looked past Quinn to Alex and sent her a wistful smile and nod before looking back at Quinn and asking, "What are you guys doing here?"

Quinn's face hardened again. "We need your help."

Chapter Ten

Cooper had led them through the dim warehouse to a staff break room that was brightly lit with several lanterns. They all took a seat around a long table and filled him in on what had been happening in their town.

Josh leaned forward in his seat. "What's the leadership here like? Do you think they would be willing to trade for the meds we need?"

Cooper rubbed at his mouth thoughtfully before replying. "Colonel Tremble seems like a fair man but he's also made some hard rules. They won't accept any new refugees until spring and everyone here over ten years old has to work or they don't eat. They've been very tight with the rations lately and medicine is one of the things they don't have a huge supply of. I honestly don't know if he would trade with you."

Josh sat back with a frustrated sigh. "Yeah, apparently the town council had contact with him on the radio when the virus first hit. He told them to quarantine and ride it out. He wasn't willing to part with any medicine no matter what they offered him. Said he wanted to keep the supply in case the city got hit with it. Do you think he'd change his mind?"

Cooper shook his head. "I don't really know him that well, but like I said he's a stickler for the rules so I doubt it."

Quinn gave a hard nod and waved his hand dismissively. "I didn't figure we'd have any luck here. So let's move on. Cooper, you've been with these guys since early summer. Have they already cleaned out the bigger cities, Calgary, Edmonton?"

Cooper's eyes widened. "No, no way, man! You guys can't go all the way to Calgary or Edmonton. The cities are a death trap. Even the military stayed out of them. They planned on waiting until next summer before heading into them. That way most of the population would be dead from the cold or starvation."

Quinn just nodded and turned to the others as he pushed his chair back and got to his feet.

"Good, I was worried they might have gone in and stripped the hospitals. That means the meds should still be there." He looked down at his grandfather's watch. "Let's get going. We've wasted too much time today already."

Alex checked her own watch and saw that it was already eleven thirty. A sense of urgency overcame her now that she knew they would have a longer journey ahead of them. She had hoped they would make it home by dark, but now she knew it wouldn't be possible so the sooner they got to Calgary the faster they could get on the road tomorrow.

"I agree with Quinn. Let's get going. If we need to search multiple hospitals it will take a really long time, so the sooner we get to Calgary the better."

Everyone else except Cooper nodded and got to their feet. His bewildered face looked to each one of them until he too stood up with his hands held up in a stop motion.

"You guys aren't seriously going to go all the way to Calgary in the dead of winter to look for something that's probably already been looted, are you?"

Emily looked him dead in the eye and asked, "Are you willing to steal the medicine we need from here?"

When he shook his head "no", she shrugged.

"Then, yes, we are. Just like we crossed a broken country to get home. Sailed a dead ocean and fought and killed a gang of thugs to save our families. A little trip down the highway to find medicine for people who are dying isn't that challenging. Maybe living here has made you too comfortable or have you forgotten what it means to fight for the people who matter to you?"

Cooper's face flushed red at such words coming from the sweet girl he remembered her to be and realized that not just Quinn had changed. He looked at the determined faces around him and it reminded him of what he had felt when he had fought by their side not that long ago. The past few months had been easy and comfortable in some ways, but the time had left him feeling empty and without purpose. Squaring his shoulders, he cleared his throat.

"You're right. I thought staying here and joining up with the military would make me useful. The truth is, we haven't really done anything to help people except give them busy work to keep them occupied. During the summer there was farming and outreach to other communities but since the harvest they've locked this area down and don't let anyone in or out. They don't help when radio calls come in either. All we do here now is go house to house, business to business and strip them clean of anything useful and then store them. I know they plan on building even more greenhouses in the spring and planting more crops but I haven't heard anything about them having plans to help out the rest of the province or country. Don't get me wrong, they aren't overlords or anything like that, but they have everything they need right here with all the supplies and an easily controlled workforce to do all the farming. I think this is it for them. I thought I would be helping more people if I stayed. What they're doing here is a good thing but it's kind of a let down to what I was expecting."

They all stood looking at him expectantly so he let out another deep breath. "If you'll have me, I'll come and help."

Josh's face split into a grin and Emily gave him a cool nod but Alex reached across the table for his hand.

"Of course we'll have you, Cooper! It wouldn't be the Maple Leaf Mafia without you!"

Before he could reply, Quinn barked out, "Alex!" and grabbed the arm she had reached out to Cooper. He pulled her away from the table and through the door of the staff room. As soon as the door had swung shut behind her, she wrenched her arm from his grip and whirled to face him with a furious expression.

"How dare you! Who do you think you are?" She practically spit at him in contempt.

His expression was full of frustration when he said, "Do you really want to go down that path again? You broke the guy's heart the last time he was with us!"

Alex barked out an incredulous laugh. "Yeah, because I chose YOU! Clearly that was the wrong choice! I might have broken Cooper's heart but you broke mine so you have NO say in what I now choose to do or who I hang out with." She reached up and tugged the chain around her neck until it broke and then held out the ring that he had given her until he finally took it.

"Just go home, Quinn. I don't need you anymore."

Alex spun away, yanked the door back open and sailed through it without a backward glance so she didn't see Quinn's face crumple with grief.

Dead silence greeted her when she entered the room and everyone except Cooper kept their gazes away from her. He stood tall and his expression was fierce.

"I would like to join you on the trip to Calgary but I don't want to cause a rift between you and Quinn."

Alex's shoulder's slumped wearily and she tiredly shook her head.

"Cooper, I would love for you to join us. There's already a rift in place between Quinn and I and it has nothing to do with you."

She felt the draft from the door behind her opening and stiffened at Quinn's voice. "She's right Cooper. It has nothing to do with you. It would be good to have another fighter with us if things go sideways in the city. You're welcome to join us."

Cooper stared hard over Alex's shoulder before finally giving a brisk nod. "Alright, then let's go." He broke eye contact with Quinn and turned to Josh.

"I don't really know if they'd let me leave so it might be better if I just slipped away. I'll need to go grab some gear from my barracks and change out of this uniform. Where's a good place to meet up with you?"

Josh filled him in on where they had stashed their sleds. They agreed that it would be best if the group left the same way they had come in and Cooper would slip out of town from a different area. He knew where all the sentries and road blocks were placed so he shouldn't have any problem slipping through.

They left the warehouse by the front entrance and went separate ways. As the main group worked their way back the way they had come, they noticed that things had changed in the short time since they had passed through. Earlier, people had been milling about all over the place. Now, everyone was standing in long, semi-organized lines waiting to get into different buildings. Every person in a line was holding a bowl and a plate. Alex guessed it must be lunchtime. That was confirmed when a few people started to come out of the doors with steaming bowls of what looked like thin watery soup. They all clutched their bowls tightly and avoided looking at the hungry people eyeing them from the lines. It almost seemed like they were afraid that someone would rush them and steal their food.

Alex could only say a thankful prayer as they passed by that none of her loved ones were forced to live in such conditions. Hard stares met them as they passed by the many lines but no one spoke to them or tried to stop them. It was a huge relief to finally round the bend and come to the empty stretch before the roadblock in the distance.

The soldiers that had let them past earlier were still in place. They looked hopefully at Alex to see if she would part with any more of the home baked goods that Josh's mom had sent but she just nodded and moved past them. The fight with Quinn was weighing heavily on her shoulders. Her emotions kept bouncing back and forth between fury and despair.

The head soldier who had made the decision to let them pass earlier called out. "That didn't take very long! Didn't you find your friend?"

Josh nodded at him but kept moving. "Yeah, we found him. He just wasn't as interested in visiting as we had hoped. No point sticking around wasting time."

The soldier frowned with a knowing expression. "That's too bad. This world we have now, it changes people. It was nice of you guys to try and look him up. You all have a safe trip home and maybe we'll see you again this spring."

Josh just nodded and gave him a sloppy salute before trudging on through the snow away from the roadblocks.

Dara fell back and murmured a few words to him. He nodded and picked up his pace until he was up in the lead with Quinn. Emily, Lisa and Dara flanked Alex and slowed their pace down until there was a decent gap between them and the boys.

Emily was the first to speak. "Are you okay, Alex?"

Alex narrowed her eyes and gritted her teeth. "I'm FINE!" She snapped and stomped her next step into the snow.

Dara made an "hmm" noise and that's all it took to open the floodgates for Alex.

"Seriously, seriously? Who does he think he is? I certainly don't know who he is anymore! As if he thought he had any right to speak to me about Cooper! Argggg!"

Emily patted her on the back sympathetically. "Well, if you and Quinn are finished, Cooper clearly still has feelings for you."

Alex angrily shook her head. "This is like a big joke! Every time we have something important to do, the universe has to throw in boy drama? Why does this keep happening to me?"

Lisa cocked her head and kicked at the snow in front of her before speaking. "You know, it is kind of funny."

Alex sent her a harsh look and spat, "FUNNY?"

Lisa nodded slowly then went off in a rapid-fire rant. "Yeah, it goes like this, Boy meets girl. Girl bosses him around for ten years. Apocalypse happens. Boy declares love for girl. Girl's like, yeah but look at this other boy, he's cute.

Other boy's like "How you doing?" she said in a Joey Tribbiani parody from the Friends TV show voice. "Girl finally chooses boy. Other boy leaves with a broken heart. First boy turns into a jerk. Other boy's back with "How you doing?" Girl has enough and shoots both boy and other boy. Problem solved!"

The three girls stared at Lisa incredulously until a snort finally escaped from Alex. Her snort turned into a gasping half laugh that then turned into a full-on belly laugh and caused the other girls to break out into their own laughter. The girls laughed so hard that they ended up just sitting down in the snow.

Josh and Quinn stop and turn back to watch the girls. The confused expressions on their faces caused the girls to just laugh even harder until they all gasped for breath.

Dara was the first to recover and catch her breath. She wiped the tears of laughter from her face and gave Alex a semi-serious look.

"Listen, Alex. In the big, overall picture of things right now? The two boy-crazy is nothing. They'll figure it out or you will, but it's not life or death. All that really matters right now and IS life or death, is our mission. We have to find the medicine to save our town and no boy drama is worth getting in the way of that."

Alex looked at her friends and nodded with a better attitude. "You're absolutely right. None of that matters at all compared to what we have to do." She rubbed hard at her face. "God, sometimes I feel so old and then I remember I'm only eighteen! I hopefully have years to figure out who I'm going to spend my life with." She rose up to her feet and helped pull her friends to theirs. "Come on, let's get this done."

They all shared a hug before turning and moving up and then past the boys who still stood looking at them in confusion. As Lisa passed them she shot Quinn a wink.

"Come on, Boy. We have a town to save!"

When he heard the other three girls giggle, Josh just shook his head with bemusement and muttered, "I will NEVER understand women!"

By the time they made it back to the burned-out office building, Cooper was waiting for them. He had changed out of his uniform but still wore a camouflaged snow parka. There was a pack at his feet and a military issued rifle hanging on a sling from his shoulder.

No words were spoken as he hefted his pack and fell into line as they made their way around the building to where they had stashed their sleds and the Ranger. Cooper's eyes flared wide in surprise when Josh pulled the tarp off of the new UTV.

"Man, I'm not even all that surprised you found something like this. I mean, I had some long boring nights when I was laid up healing from that gunshot wound to think about our trip home from Cali. Do you realize just how incredibly lucky we were? Think about all the supplies we managed to get right off the bat and then we just stumble on not one but two working vehicles. We crossed a country that was full on anarchy, made it home then managed to free our town from roughly one hundred gang members. All with none of us dying. There's an Angel watching over this group!"

Josh just shrugged and smirked. "OR, I'm just that good!"

Dara bumped him aside with her hip and tossed her pack onto the front seat. "OR, we can NOT tempt fate by saying thank you to whoever or whatever is looking over us. Oh, and, shotgun!"

Josh looked up to the sky, raised his hands and mouthed the words thank you before turning to the others.

"Okay, who wants to ride with me and my babe in style and who's going to be eating the wind?"

Alex wanted some time alone so she secured her pack in the trailer of the sled she had driven here and climbed on waiting for the others to get sorted. Emily and Lisa decided to ride in the UTV with Josh and Dara so that left Quinn and Cooper to drive the other two sleds. They had already mapped out what roads they were going to take to loop around Red Deer and avoid any more road blocks before hooking back up to the main highway that ran straight into Calgary.

It was an easy ride in the warming temperatures and it got warmer the further south they traveled. Alex had always marveled over how the temperature could change by ten to fifteen degrees in as little as one hundred kilometres in her province. She knew it had something to do with how the mountains channelled the wind but not exactly why. All she cared about right now was that they were headed to even warmer weather. She just hoped that the temperature was the only thing hot they were headed towards.

Chapter Eleven

There were exactly nine exits from the highway between the two cities and Alex figured if trouble was waiting for them it would most likely be at one of those exits. The one-hundred-and-thirty-kilometer stretch was wide open prairie that let them see for miles. A few gentle rises along the way but with hardly any trees, it left the big divided highway open to the wind. Before the lights went out, this stretch could be treacherous in the winter causing many huge pile-ups every year. With no natural windbreaks, the blowing snow would pile up in drifts when it wasn't causing deadly black ice.

Cooper had told them that the military had moved all the stranded vehicles off the highway as far south as the town of Bowden but stopped there, planning to continue clearing the main artery sometime in the coming summer. It made for a smooth forty-kilometer ride for the group until that town and then the real challenges began. With cars, trucks and many transport trailers scattered all over the highway, it was a minefield of massive snow drifts of all different heights. Add to that the warmth of the chinook making the snow unstable and they ended up having no choice but to leave the highway's surface and drive in the more stable ditches and secondary service roads that ran parallel to it. Of the five towns between Bowden and Calgary all but the last one was set five to ten kilometres west of the highway. It was also the worst stretch of the trip, before and after lights out. What would have been an easy hour-and-ten-minute drive before, now took them almost two-and-a-half hours due to the slower speeds and having to constantly work their way around obstacles.

By the time they reached the last town before Calgary, they were all exhausted from the tense ride. They pulled over at Josh's arm waving out the window and shut down their machines. When Alex swung her leg over her sled's seat to dismount she staggered a few steps away on noodle-like legs. Cooper was closest to her and grabbed her arm to steady her. He helped her take off her helmet and brushed a few sweaty red curls back from her face.

Alex gave him a tentative smile but seeing Quinn's stony face over his shoulder had her turning away from them both with an eye roll to dig out her pack and water bottle. She guzzled down half of it in one go before looking over at the rest of her friends.

Lisa was also unsteady as her feet hit the snow and her face was pale. She met Alex's eyes and shook her head.

"Ride in style, he said! Yeah, if style means almost tipping over like twenty times! I'm not getting back into that thing again. Alex, can I ride with you the rest of the way, pleeeeease?" she begged.

Josh threw his hands in the air as he climbed out. "I had complete control the whole time!"

Lisa shot him a look like he was insane and moved further away from him and the UTV. Alex just laughed and handed the girl what was left of the water.

Josh just shrugged. "Whatever! So that's Airdrie ahead. It's a decent sized suburb city. The highway cuts right through it. After that, it's straight into Calgary. Does everyone agree to try the Foothills Hospital first? If that doesn't pan out, the Sick Kid's is just down the road from it. If we strike out at both of those, we're going to have to find shelter for the night. The other hospitals are too far to make today."

When everyone had nodded or verbally agreed, he continued. "All right, then lets…"

Alex threw up her hand and cocked her head to the side. She took two strides past him and scanned the field to the west. Everyone else turned to look that way to see what she was looking at. Dara stepped into the UTV while hanging on to the roll bar to give herself more height, pointed into the field in the distance.

"There, three snowmobiles headed south into Airdrie on the next road over!"

Josh rushed over to the cargo bed and opened his pack bringing out a pair of binoculars. He hopped up into the cargo bed and panned the area Dara had pointed out.

"Uh, guys? They're stopping and looking this way!" Dara called out. "Now they're pointing this way! Annnnnd, they're moving again!"

Josh jumped down muttering "Crap, crap, crap!"

Everyone could hear the high revs of the engines across the field as the other three sleds raced towards town faster than they had been before spotting them. It either meant they were scared of them or they were coming for them.

Josh quickly zipped up his pack and tossed the binoculars onto the seat.

"Alex, help me pull the rifles out and pass them around. I don't know if those guys are headed our way or not but we should gear up now. We should have our AK's out before we hit Calgary anyway. Anyone who has to heed Mother Nature's call should get on that too. Once we get to the outskirts of the city, we probably shouldn't stop again if we can help it. With over a million people pre EMP, there's bound to be some still left looking for trouble."

He passed out the assault rifles along with extra magazines of ammunition that had traveled with them all the way from southern Utah where they had taken them from a biker gang. As soon as everyone had a rifle and taken a quick bathroom break they loaded up. They kept their speed up as much as they could with all the obstacles in the way. Whoever the other group was or their intentions, they wanted to get as far away from them as possible.

With a day of warmer weather, the snow on many of the stranded cars and trucks had started to melt letting patches of shiny metal roofs show through. Alex had to concentrate on her driving but when she occasionally glanced back she could see Dara, Lisa and Emily scanning in all directions from the Ranger. She let out a relieved breath when they finally passed the last commercial building at the small city's edge and open fields were all she could see ahead, but they continued to keep the speed up for a few more kilometres.

On the east side of the highway was a huge outlet mall that they had all shopped at before. It was anchored by a massive outdoor hunting and fishing store and Alex wondered if they should stop there on the way back. Remembering that Calgary was only a few miles away she realized that the place would have been stripped bare if even a fraction of the city's population had headed this way.

Once they passed the mall and the exit for the city bypass, they had no choice but to slow right down. The road was filled with snow covered vehicles - more vehicles than they had seen since they had traveled out of the Los Angeles area. Alex thought back on the timing of the EMP and remembered that it had happened pretty early in the morning. All these cars would have been in the morning rush hour carrying commuters to work. When they came upon a jackknifed transport trailer they left the road completely and drove down the center median.

It was four lanes of snow buried cars going into the city but the outgoing lanes weren't as congested, so they slowly wound their way back and forth from the median to the northbound lanes as they watched the exit signs for the route they would take to get to the first two hospitals on their list. Alex was concentrating on the road but still kept looking to either side of the highway for signs of survivors. So far, the sky had been free of smoke trails and she hadn't seen any movement to suggest that there was anyone living nearby. It was incredibly lonely knowing that less than a year ago, this area was a bustling city that had action twenty-four hours a day.

Josh's UTV pulled up even with her sled and he pointed to a sign coming up on the southbound lanes. She squinted her eyes and saw that it was announcing the exit they needed in two kilometres. She slowed slightly and let him take the lead as they crept closer to it. It was only minutes later that the UTV started to slow and then came to a stop. Alex pulled up beside it and looked at Josh to see why he stopped. The look on his face was one of amazed horror. She followed his line of sight but couldn't see what had given him such a reaction so she shut her machine off and pulled off her helmet to get a better look at what was ahead. She stepped up onto the seat of her snowmobile and just gazed in astonishment at what blocked their way.

The overpass bridge ahead of them had been sheared off, leaving jagged concrete ledges on both sides of the highway and a mound of rubble covering all of the southbound and most of the northbound lanes. On the west side, where a four-lane street should have been, was a massive crater. The snow had melted enough for the tail fin of a passenger plane to be seen. Alex shook her head at the destruction. This was the second plane she had seen that had crashed the day of the EMP. The first one had been on their trip out of the LA area and it had crashed into a shopping mall causing a huge, out of control fire.

Cooper's voice rang out in the stillness. "Hey, Josh? That was our exit, right?"

Alex turned away from the twisted rebar and concrete chunks and looked up at the sky. There was a clock ticking away in her head that got louder with every delay in their trip.

"Yeah, we'll have to either go around this mess or backtrack. The next exit is Memorial Drive. It skirts around downtown on this side of the river and we can take it all the way to Crowchild Trail then back north to where the Foothills hospital is. If we go back to the last exit we would be traveling on smaller side streets through residential areas."

The ticking grew a little louder in Alex's head so she just waved her arm forward.

"Let's go to the next one. We're going to run out of daylight soon and I don't want to be searching an abandoned hospital in the dark!" She didn't wait for an answer, just pulled her helmet back on, straddled her sled seat and fired it back up.

She let Quinn take the lead this time with Josh following her and Cooper in the rear. As they slowly made their way around the destruction, Alex's mind went to the conflicting emotions she was feeling. On the one hand, she was happy to be away from the farm and her parent's questioning looks and the pity that she saw on their faces since she had her outburst. On the other hand, she hated that they were probably frantic with worry over her leaving on what they would think was a too dangerous trip for their little girl. She sighed deeply, causing her helmet visor to fog up and gave a small laugh at herself. She was tired of feeling torn between her parents and her freedom, not to mention the stupid boy issue!

The trapped feeling she had felt over the past few months had eased off since they had made the decision to go on this trip, but it was only a bandage to the problems she faced back home. If she wanted to be treated like an adult, then she would have to buck up and make some adult decisions. As much as she loved her family and Quinn, she had to decide for herself how she was going to go forward from here once they made it home. The EMP had broken more than civilization when it had gone off that day. It broke the mold on how and when children would grow up and the life they would lead.

Her thoughts were interrupted when they were once again forced to stop. They had navigated the destroyed overpass and made it to the next exit and up off the freeway but the street leading into downtown was packed with vehicles that had been caught in the morning rush hour. Alex fumed at yet another delay but shut her machine down as well and waited as Josh and Quinn went on foot ahead to see if they could find a path through the mess blocking them.

Cooper walked over to her and pulled off his helmet. "You doing ok?"

She flipped her visor up and nodded. "Yeah, just frustrated with all this. I don't know why I thought it would be easy to navigate the city. We saw the aftermath when we biked out of the Los Angeles area. A million people means a lot of dead cars on the road." She took a sip from a water bottle he handed to her. "I'm just anxious to get the meds our people need."

Cooper nodded and looked at the view of the many skyscraper buildings that made up the downtown core and sighed.

"I'm sorry I didn't try and contact you guys before this. Once I was healed, I thought about traveling back to Prairie Springs but I just thought it would be for the best if I stayed away. After what my dad did to the town and with you and Quinn together, well, I just didn't want to cause any problems."

Alex scowled. "Cooper, you're an idiot!" When his face bloomed with surprise, she shook her head in exasperation. "Seriously? You are not your dad! You helped free our town and took a bullet for them. And as for me and Quinn, you being there or not didn't make any difference to our problems! You crossed the country with us to get home and we are a family, no matter who's dating who or where you are!" She took a deep breath to continue but the grin on his face had her sputtering, "What are you smiling about?"

He shrugged as his grin got wider. "Just you. I missed your rapid-fire rants against injustice." He let out a laugh. "I just missed you, period!"

Alex could feel the heat creeping into her cheeks at his words so she looked away and shrugged. "Well, we missed you too. What were you doing in Red Deer anyway?"

He snorted. "Basically, a whole lot of nothing! Once I was healed and I joined up, mostly grunt work. They had these huge scavenging parties go house to house and strip them of everything useful. Right down to the windows for more greenhouses. Then it was just sort and store. Once spring hits, they plan on expanding and bringing in more survivors. They'll control everything in that area, including the people. I know rebuilding is going to be hard but I honestly didn't feel like I was helping anyone. It kind of felt like a prison to me. Not that they were abusive to the refugees but it was pretty strict compared to the way things used to be. Lots of rules, schedules and rationing."

Alex wrinkled her nose. "That sounds awful but at least those people are safe and fed. There are probably a lot of people who would give anything to have that right now." A thought made her face change to alarm. "Hey! They aren't going to force people to relocate there, are they?"

Cooper shook his head. "I didn't hear anything like that. It was just opening the gates for more people to come in this spring. They'll want as many as they can get to plant crops and build the greenhouses so they can grow year-round. I can't see them forcing people who have a good set up like Prairie Springs to move."

Alex huffed out a breath. "Wouldn't that just take the cake? After everything we been through and all the fighting. Can you imagine having all of it taken away by the one group that's supposed to protect us?"

Before Cooper could respond, Josh and Quinn came back and the other girls joined them. Josh guzzled water from the bottle Dara handed to him and then passed it to Quinn as he explained their next moves.

"So, this on ramp is right buggered! BUT, all is not lost. In between the east and westbound bridges are the light rail transit train tracks. They look clear as far as the next station. There might be a train sitting in the station but I doubt both sides of the tracks are blocked. We just need to head a little bit east to where the cement barrier ends then hop on the train bridge." He bit his lip in worry while looking from face to face. "So, slight concern. Each track has its own elevated skinny bridge for about a hundred feet. Not a lot of room for error. Also, with the snow melt, there won't be a lot of padding between us and the tracks so it might be a bumpy ride. But after that, we're back on solid ground and we can hopefully make some better time using the tracks to stay away from the congested roads. Any questions?"

Everyone but Quinn stared at him in disbelief so he shrugged and grinned.

"What? I mean, yeah it's a little tricky, but it's doable and there's what looks like cement guardrails so we *should* be fine." When their expressions didn't change, his shoulders slumped. "We either do it here or we head further away from where we need to be and then backtrack. That'll add on even more time and we'll have to cut through the core of downtown."

Alex looked at her friends and saw their discouraged expressions. It had already been a long day full of obstacles and roadblocks. She wasn't going to add another one to it.

"Let's do it! We knew it wouldn't be easy. So, let's just take it nice and slow on the train bridge and move on already."

Emily nodded her agreement. "Alex's right. We don't know what we'll find at the next exit or how bad the core will be. We could spend the rest of the day just trying to get through it. At least here there's a path forward. We just need to take it slow and be careful."

Josh looked around at all the others and received nods of agreement so he waved his arm forward. "All right then, onward!"

Chapter Twelve

Everyone climbed back on their machines and started them up. They worked their way slowly through the vehicles until they came to the intersection on top of the overpass that gave them an opening to the train tracks. For the first twenty feet of the tracks they were on the overpass and the snow was piled up almost level with the guardrails but at the start of the train bridge, the snow had melted in places leaving the tracks bare of snow but still icy.

Josh led the way with the UTV. The body of the machine and the Sno-Cobra ski and track attachments were wide enough to straddle the train tracks and avoid the raised metal lines completely. Other than a few bumps from where the wood ties were bare, he had no problem driving over the bridge at all. Everyone else's snowmobiles would have to navigate inside the metal lines and try not to get hung up on them.

Alex nudged her sled forward on to the tracks and kept a tight grip on her steering. She made it halfway across the bridge before a slight curve in the track had her front left ski scraping against the metal rail. The jolt of it made her overcorrect and caused her right ski to connect on the other side. She squeezed the brakes to come to a stop and took a deep breath before straightening up and moving forward again. She was going so slow that she worried the machine would stall out on her, but she finally made it off the bridge where the tracks leveled out on solid ground. The snow had blown or melted away on this section of track so Josh and the girls helped her lift the front end of the sled to the side and then the back end and trailer off the tracks completely so she could drive on the embankment.

As they watched the other two sleds drive towards them on the bridge, Alex talked to Josh about something she was worried about.

"If the snow is melting all over the city, we won't be able to drive very far with our sleds. If we have to go on foot it could take us days to walk everywhere we need to go!"

Josh kept his eyes on Quinn and Cooper as they slowly crept towards them over the bridge but nodded his head.

"Yeah, I thought about that too. I'm hoping it won't come to that. This area's wide open so that's probably why the snow melted here faster in places but it shouldn't be like this all over the city. Worst case scenario? We would have to swap the ski and tracks back to the tires on the UTV and split up. We'd have to find a safe place for half of us to wait with the snowmobiles while four of us use the UTV to get to the hospitals."

Alex's frown deepened. "I don't like the idea of us splitting up at all! There's too many unknowns with what's happening in this city. We haven't even seen any survivors yet. We could be driving into trouble as it is. Splitting up is a really bad idea."

Josh let out a worried sigh. "I agree so let's just hope we can find a way through."

Once Quinn and Cooper had made it over the bridge and joined them, they all worked to lift the guy's sleds and trailers off the tracks. Alex turned and looked further west down the line towards the downtown core, then looked up at the late afternoon sky. Daylight would be gone soon. That meant things were about to get even harder.

The group started out again and headed towards the station that was less than a kilometer away. Josh took the lead again but there was plenty of room beside and between the two sets of tracks for everyone to stay close together. The snow deepened again as they moved away from the overpass making the sleds ride smoother for everyone. The platforms for the station were outside, exposed to the elements, and no trains blocked the way ahead.

Once they got close enough, Alex could see the signs above the station that read, ZOO. She had a sad pang at the thought of all those animals trapped in their cages and left to die when the lights went out. That thought was quickly followed by the concern that the zookeepers might have let them all out to roam the city. She couldn't help but scan around the area for a lion ready to pounce on them which is why she saw movement inside the glass station overlooking the platform they were about to reach.

Alex yelled out for them to stop as she spotted more shapes moving behind the glass. They weren't going very fast so it only took seconds for the group to come to a stop and when they saw Alex jump off her sled and bring her rifle around on its sling they all followed suit. At the same time, four men barrelled out of the glass doors at the end of the station. They each held a weapon pointed at the group of teens. They had come to a stop just past the end of the platform so Alex could clearly see that one man had a shotgun, one had a bolt action rifle and two had handguns pointed at them. Even though the men had the higher ground, the seven assault rifles pointed at them more than evened the playing field.

The older man holding the shotgun had an angry expression and stabbed it towards them as he barked out,

"Get out of here! We told you people what would happen the next time you came around. Did you think we were bluffing?"

Josh spared a quick look at his friends and then took a half step forward. "Yeah, I don't think we got the memo on that. We live over two hundred klicks north of here and this is the first time we've been to the city since lights out. So if you don't mind, we'll just keep on going that-a-way." He pointed past the station towards downtown.

One of the men pointing a handgun snorted a disbelieving laugh but the older man just scowled at them and shook his head.

"Yeah, nice try. Nobody travels that kind of distance anymore. Especially not in the worst winter we've ever seen!"

Alex rolled her eyes and gritted her teeth. This was just one more obstacle in the way of them getting the meds their people needed. She was out of patience. She flipped her visor up.

"Listen, Mister! I'm sorry for whatever troubles you have here with other people but it's not us! We just need to get past here to find what we're here for. It's been a long day of traveling and the sun's going to be down soon so we need to move on. We have no interest in or fight with you or your people and we'll leave the city a different way when we get what we came for."

The man squinted down at her and surprise filled his face. "You're just a girl!"

Alex let that comment go and his scowl lessened slightly to a frown. "Let's say I believe you? Where you coming from and what are you after? It's been a long time since we've seen anyone from out of the city so any news would be welcome."

Alex huffed out an impatient breath. "I don't care if you believe me or not. We don't have time for a chat and I'm not the CBC News! In case you didn't notice, our guns are bigger than yours so..."

Josh interrupted her. "Uh, Alex? We actually should have a chat with these guys. They probably have information we can use to get where we're going."

Alex bit the inside of her cheek hard to stop herself from screeching out her frustration. She knew Josh was right but the ticking clock in her head was telling her to keep moving. She clenched her teeth and grunted out, "FINE!"

Josh stared at her in concern until she finally nodded, lowered her weapon and took a step back. He turned away from her and addressed the men above them.

"So, if we're going to parley can we all lower the boom boom sticks?"

A grin tugged at the older man's mouth and he started to nod. "Lower your weapons, men."

Everyone except Alex relaxed their stance as Josh told a condensed version of their story.

"We come from a small town an hour west of Red Deer. The town's been hit hard by some kind of sickness and a lot of people have died. We all live on farms outside of the town so none of us has been exposed. When the chinook hit, we decided to make a run to Red Deer with the hope that the military would give us the medicine our doctor said our town needs. When they wouldn't help, we had no choice but to come here where there are more hospitals and medical clinics to search. Alex is right about it being a long day and we're all worried about how long it will take to find what we need and get back home. We also don't know how long the chinook is going to last. It'll be brutal if we get caught on the road when the temperature drops again."

The three men started calling out questions as soon as Josh finished speaking but the older man held up his hand to silence them.

"I'd like to hear more about the military. We haven't seen or heard from anyone in the government since this all began. We also have some firsthand information about the hospitals in this area." He looked up at the sky and frowned before continuing. "It'll be dark in less than an hour. You don't want to be traveling through the city at night. Especially since the warm up." As if to punctuate his words, a distant gunshot rang out. The man's face went grim and he nodded.

"There's a lot of decent people spread out in the city who are just trying to survive but there's even more savage animals looking to destroy. With the warmer temperatures, they'll be out in full force tonight. If your group doesn't know the ins and outs of the city, then you probably won't make it out alive. Even with your big boom boom sticks, as you call them. I would like to offer your group shelter for the night in exchange for information and news. I can guarantee your safety with us and also provide you the route to take and what the hospitals are like right now. A few of our people traveled to them not that long ago."

Josh rubbed at his chin in thought and then held up a finger to ask for a minute. When the man nodded, Josh turned to his friends and they all gathered around to discuss the offer.

Alex took a deep breath to launch into her reasoning to reject the offer and keep going when a distant explosion rang through the air. They all turned in the direction it had come from and saw in the dimming light a smoke cloud billowing up from in between two of the office buildings in the core.

Cooper was the first to speak. "Holy crap, it's like a war zone in there! I vote we stay and get the best way to avoid all that."

Dara chimed in with Emily and Lisa nodding in agreement. "He's right. It'll be dark pretty quick and I don't want to go anywhere near that!"

Quinn just shrugged at Josh's questioning look so he turned to Alex. "I know you want to blaze through and get to where we need to be but we won't be helping our town if we end up dead. These people seem to feel safe here and the city is their turf so they'll know the best way for us to go. This might actually save us time in the long run. And Alex, we do have to sleep eventually so this might be the safest place to do that."

Alex looked around at her friend's expressions and saw that they all agreed with Josh so she just gave a curt nod and turned away. It was the best thing to do but she didn't have to like it. She heard him sigh at her attitude and then call out to the other group.

"We'd like to take you up on your offer. Where exactly is your shelter?"

Alex turned so she saw the old man grin before replying. "It's in the Zoo!"

Chapter Thirteen

There was no easy way for them to get their sleds and trailers into the zoo from where they were. The glass station had dead escalators and a steep stairway that led underground to where the main entrance to the park was. The older man introduced himself as Matthew and sent one of the other men to ride on the back of Cooper's sled, they backtracked on the tracks until they cleared the platforms and concrete barriers. It was quick work with bolt cutters to create an opening in the chain link fence big enough for them to drive through and onto the eastbound lanes. The street leading out of the core wasn't as heavily congested with dead vehicles as the westbound lanes so they had no problem navigating through. They drove the sleds up the embankment to another chain link fence that surrounded the zoo grounds. This fence was carefully cut along a support post and peeled back before the man that gave his name as Jeff re-secured it with zip ties after they had driven through.

Jeff gave them directions through the grounds as the sounds of their engines brought curious people out of buildings they passed. The people followed behind them as they drove over a bridge and into the main zoo grounds. All the exterior cages and enclosures that Alex could see were empty of living or dead animals and she once again wondered what had happened to them. Jeff had them pull up in front of a large glass-topped building and shut their machines down.

A large group of around thirty people was starting to surround them with more joining as they caught up. The group of teens dismounted and pulled their helmets off. Alex was starting to get nervous with the way the people were eyeing the snowmobiles and trailers covered with tarps. She edged closer to her friends and her hand started to reach back towards her rifle when a loud voice rang out.

"Everyone back up! Give these people room."

Alex relaxed slightly when the crowd took a few steps back and started to part to let through the owner of the voice. She tensed back up again when she felt someone tightly grip her arm. Whipping her head around she was surprised to see it was Lisa clutching her and the girl's face was deathly pale. Alex was about to ask her what was wrong when the voice started yelling again so she turned back and saw a good looking middle aged man with a young, heavily pregnant woman on his arm break free of the crowd.

"I know Matthew offered you shelter here for the night but he doesn't have the authority to do that! I'm sorry but we don't know you or know your intentions. We can't compromise our group's safety."

Just then, Matthew walked through the crowd and gave the man with the loud voice a hard look.

"It's also not for you to decide if they stay, Kirkland! I spoke to these people and determined they aren't a threat. They've traveled a great distance and have news of the government."

The man, Kirkland, scoffed. "And you just believed them? For all you know they could be spies for one of the gangs. Sent here to infiltrate our group and steal our food and women and then kill the rest of us!"

Before anyone else could speak, Lisa pushed through from behind her friends and pulled her hat off. She zeroed in on Kirkland and stared at him with one of her ice queen death stares.

"We don't want your food or your women but I do know someone who would like to kill you! Then again, she probably doesn't even remember your face but I'd take a shot at killing you myself!"

The crowd gasped and the man's mouth dropped open in disbelief as he managed to gasp, "Lisa?"

Lisa raised her eyebrows in contempt. "Hi Dad, you asshole!"

Matthew worked hard at not smiling but his eyes danced with merriment when he asked, "So, I take it you know these people?"

Kirkland was still open mouthed when the lady on his arm tugged at it. "Kirky, who is that girl?"

He started shaking his head. "Lisa, my daughter." He shook her off his arm and stepped towards Lisa. "But where, how, what are you doing here?"

There was no thaw in her face when she shrugged. "It certainly wasn't to find my deadbeat Dad! This is just an unhappy coincidence."

He took another step as shame filled his face and he started pleading. "Honey, you don't understand! I couldn't make it home. That day, you have no idea what it was like here in the city on that day! Nothing worked, people went crazy. Planes dropped from the sky! You and your mother were safe in Prairie Springs away from the big city populations. You have no idea what I went through!"

Lisa's mouth started to twitch and then her expression cracked when she heard Emily snicker behind her. When a small laugh escaped Alex and then Dara, she couldn't hold back and she gasped out a full-on laugh causing all her friends to laugh too.

Her father's face went from pleading to confusion to anger and he finally couldn't take it anymore. "What is wrong with you? How dare you laugh at my misery? There was nothing I could do to get back to you and your mother! For God's sake Lisa, it's over two hundred kilometres. No one could make that!"

Lisa wiped away a tear of laughter and nodded her head in understanding. "Yeah, that's really, really, REALLY FAR!" The laughter left her face and the ice queen came back. "I was in Los Angeles Father, I made it home."

Her dad shook his head. "What are you talking about?"

Lisa let out an exhausted sigh and waved her hand dismissively.

"Class trip? No? Hmmm, didn't even know where your only child was? Yup, that pretty much sums up your parenting history. So let me catch you up! I was on a class trip to Los Angeles the day the lights went out. All of us here were. So yeah, I saw the planes fall from the sky and I was in a city of over twenty million people that went crazy. We managed to travel two thousand, five hundred kilometres to get home but yeah, I totally get how you couldn't make it home. It's really far from here! Whatever!"

She turned her back to him and walked towards her friends, her real family.

"Lisa, please! I'm sorry!"

Alex gave the man a look of disgust before turning to Matthew. "So are we staying or are we leaving?"

He gave her a firm nod. "You and your friends are more than welcome to stay here as our guests. We are all anxious to hear the news of the rest of the world. Let me show you where you will be sleeping so you can freshen up before supper."

Alex shot a look at Josh who only nodded so she replied. "I'm not comfortable leaving our sleds and supplies out here in the open. Is there somewhere more secure we can put them for the night?"

He gave a sad smile of understanding. "Yes, there's a maintenance garage not far from here where they'll be safe. I would also ask that you leave your heavy weapons there before joining us. They're a little intimidating and might frighten some of our children."

Before Alex could disagree, Quinn stepped forward. "That's fine." He turned to his group. "We'll stand a watch in the garage. Two people, four-hour shifts through the night." Everyone but Alex nodded in agreement and Matthew frowned.

"I can assure you, that's not necessary. No one here would steal from you."

Quinn turned back and found Lisa's dad in the crowd and threw his words back at him.

"Yeah, no offence but we don't know you or know your intentions. For all we know you could try and steal our food and weapons. We already know you don't want our women but just in case..." Quinn stared Lisa's father down until the shame-filled man backed away and melted into the crowd.

Matthew stepped up and put a hand on his shoulder. "Fair enough, son. Fair enough."

Quinn turned back to his friends. "Let's get the sleds moved and set up a rotation for the night."

As they fired the sleds up to move them, Alex thought about Quinn. He had barely spoken since they had their blowout in Red Deer. It was good to see him start opening up again. He used to be a huge driving force in their group and even mad at him, she missed him. She was glad he stepped up and put Lisa's father in his place. She wasn't so happy about him agreeing to leave the assault rifles with the sleds but they all carried handguns under their jackets so it was a compromise she could live with.

As they drove into a dimly lit garage, she could only hope their stop here produced information they could use to get what they needed quickly tomorrow. If all went well, they would be able to make it home by dark.

Once they had all parked off to one side of the open space and shut the machines down, they decided who would take first watch. Lisa spoke up first.

"I am more than happy to just stay here for the whole night. I have no interest in seeing or speaking with dear old deadbeat dad again!"

Cooper gave her an understanding nod and volunteered to stay with Lisa, he knew all about crappy fathers.

Quinn looked around the empty garage. "I think it would be best if we bunk right here tonight even if they offer us better accommodations. We can secure the two doors and keep a watch going through the night. I don't think we should trust them with all the supplies we brought to trade for medicine. They all look like they've been decently fed so let's save the food in case we need to trade for meds and just give them the information about what's happening outside the city. Matthew seems like an ok guy but who knows what the rest of them are like. Four working vehicles and a stack of weapons is a very tempting score, so let's just stay vigilant and hopefully there won't be any problems."

Emily jumped in with a question. "Shouldn't we offer something to contribute to supper? I mean, food in the city has to be getting scarce. For them to feed all of us, that's a big deal."

Josh nodded. "Yeah, we can give them a pork or beef roast. It won't feed all of them but it might create some extra goodwill and more than make up for anything we eat. That will still leave a lot of meat to trade if we need it. We should also pack some snow around the meat to keep it from thawing. It should still be frozen but better to be safe and keep it that way."

Emily sent him a smile of agreement. "That's sounds fair. I should check the eggs too. They're pretty protected in the travel cases but they may be all scrambled inside from the all-day ride."

Alex finally resigned herself to the delay and went over to Lisa while the others checked on the meat and eggs. Her friend was sitting sideways on one of the sleds with a lost expression on her face.

"Are you ok? That had to have been hard seeing him like that."

Lisa let out a weary sigh. "Honestly, I just don't understand how it could hurt this much. I mean, I knew my mom was a write off all along and Dad wasn't much better in a different kind of way. He always was an absent father, but to now know just how little I meant to him thrust in my face like this, well, it really sucks! Alex, he didn't even know I was on a class trip. He thought I was still at home a few hours travel from here and he didn't even *try* to come for me!"

Alex sat down beside her and put an arm around her shoulders.

"I'm so sorry Lisa. I can't even imagine how you must feel right now. I really don't understand how either of your parents could be like that. Especially now with the way the world is. Family is so important, even more so now. All I can say is that we consider you our family and nothing will ever change that. We've come too far together to ever break that bond."

Lisa wiped a tear from her cheek and leaned her head against Alex's shoulder.

"God, when I think about how I used to treat you guys. It amazes me that you just took me in like that. You guys truly are my family and I can't thank you enough for it. I didn't even know what that word was supposed to mean until this all started."

Alex just squeezed her tighter and looked to the others who had come to stand in front of them. She took a minute to just let go of all the stress that had been consuming her. To remember just how blessed she was to have each and every one of these people as her family. They all looked back at her and Lisa with the same love she was feeling.

"Are you sure you want to stay here on watch? We all have your back if you want to go and see how he's been living here."

Lisa gave a trembling smile to everyone before answering. "No, I really don't want to know. Besides, it looked like he had a pregnant woman on his arm. I have no interest in meeting his new wife." She snickered. "The first one was bad enough!"

Everyone laughed at that. Lisa's mother, Claire Kelly, was a cold self-serving woman who had forced teenage girls to work in her pleasure house. It was a move she made when a gang had taken over their town and it allowed her to have comforts and privileges no one else in town was afforded. Once the town had been freed from the gang, Claire had no remorse for the things she had done and left town without looking back, not even for her daughter.

With one last pat on the girl's shoulder, Alex got to her feet. "We'll bring you guys back something to eat."

Cooper shook his head, "Don't worry about that. I brought a bunch of rations we can have for our supper. Lisa and I will set up a sleeping area while you're gone so it'll be ready when you get back. I'm sure we'll all be ready for an early night and early start tomorrow."

Josh slapped him on the back and handed him one of Mrs. Moore's walkie talkies. "Thanks man. Good to have you back with us! Keep your radio on in case anything goes sideways."

Chapter Fourteen

Josh, Quinn, Alex, Emily and Dara left the garage and found Matthew with a small crowd waiting for them. He gave them a brief nod when he saw that they were no longer carrying their rifles and waved for them to follow him.

"We have a communal dining area where we take our meals in shifts. It's in a nice dining room that the zoo used to hold fundraising galas in. I'm sure the news of your arrival has spread by now and it will be packed with people who want to hear your story."

Alex had to ask, "What happened to all the animals?"

He gave her a sad look and shook his head. "By the time the founders of this group decided to set up a community here, most of the animals had been euthanized, freed or possibly eaten. When we got here a few weeks after lights out, the place was abandoned. Some of the exhibits like the reptiles and butterflies were still here but that was it. It took a lot of work to clean out some of the bigger animal enclosures so we could use the buildings."

Alex was sad at the thought of all those animals being put down but it was just another by-product of the devastation caused by the EMP. The group walked on empty paved paths that used to be filled with laughing children who had come to this place to be amazed and delighted by exotic animals.

Josh broached the food subject. "How do you manage to feed so many people if there are no animals?" Matthew gave him a sharp look but then relaxed when Josh followed up. "We don't want to strain your resources so we have some meat to contribute."

His face broke into a genuine smile. "That's very kind of you all. Food is one of our biggest challenges as well as fuel for heat. Once we realized that the government wasn't coming to save us we made plans to take over this area. A few of the main reasons we picked the zoo was because of the fences that secured it. The property is just over ninety-two acres and runs right down to the river so we have access to the Bow River for water and fishing for a food source.

"We knew that eventually the stores would empty and food would become the hardest resource to find. We needed to be able to grow crops, preferably year-round. The Zoo was the perfect choice for that with multiple glass conservatories already set up for the rainforest, tropical and butterfly gardens. It took a lot of work and scavenged replacement parts to bring the solar tubes and panels back on line to heat the conservatories through the winter but we got it done in time for the first freeze. All the gardens have been replaced with food crops and the rain cisterns were already in place to water everything. It was a hard go to get it all set up but we can now grow year-round.

"The biggest issue we have is a lack of protein. We do well with fishing and bird traps we set up but it's just not enough for everyone here, especially with the hard temperature drop. We eat a lot of edamame and sprouts for protein so your meat will be very welcome."

Before they could speak about anything else they came to a building with a crowd slowly moving through its doors. A ripple ran through the people waiting to get in and the teens saw at least twenty faces turning back to stare at them. Most seemed curious but a handful scowled at them like they were to blame for the world's woes.

Alex tensed up and was glad to see Quinn and Emily also go on alert. She didn't know why some of these people were unhappy with them but she was ready to defend herself and her friends if pushed to it. Hopefully it was just a mild case of stranger danger.

Matthew stopped short of the crowd with a faint frown on his face and motioned to the crowd at the door to go in. Once the people in line turned away from them and started entering the building, he let out a sigh.

"Most of these people are good and decent but a few are so filled with bitterness at what's happened that it affects every part of them. We've all lost so much but there's nothing we can do to change that. We have to go forward and try and create the best lives we can with what we've been dealt." He rubs a hand through his thinning grey hair. "I don't think you'll have any real problems but expect a dose of negativity from them. Those people are just looking for anyone to blame for what they now have to live with."

Emily snorts at his explanation. "If they're pissed at a bunch of teenagers for the end of civilization, they've got major mental issues!"

Matthew nodded. "It's not so much your age that's the issue. You just showed up with four working vehicles. It's a reminder of what we all used to have."

The bunch up at the door had cleared, but when their group moved forward to enter, Josh hung back. Once he had some distance he quickly pulled out his radio and depressed the talk button.

"Cooper, no problems yet but stay frosty. I'm getting a sled envy vibe here. Over."

The radio squelched static before Cooper's voice came through with a reply. "Frosty like ice. Watch your backs. Out."

Josh jammed the radio back into the inside chest pocket of his parka and then ran to catch up to his group. He was impressed to see the hallways leading into the dining room were dimly lit with decorative solar lawn lights. He caught up with his group just as they reached the double glass doors leading into the eating area. As soon as Matthew pulled them open, the sounds of a loud crowd flooded out to them.

Alex hesitated at the room's threshold, intimidated by so many people in one room, especially when all eyes swiveled to her and her friends. She took a deep breath and followed Matthew inside to a table that was sitting on a raised dais at one end of the room. She tried to keep her eyes forward but it didn't stop her from seeing some of the faces directed towards her. The expressions ranged from curious, hopeful, and welcoming to outright anger.

Being the center of attention like that was very uncomfortable. Alex sent a strained look down the table at her friends and saw that they were all feeling the same way she was. The crowd's noise had dimmed while they walked to the table but now it seemed to double in loudness as some people yelled questions towards them.

Matthew stood at the center of the table and raised both of his hands to try and quiet the crowd but was mostly ignored. It was the food that finally shut down the crowd.

A stern-faced woman who was standing to the side of the room at the head of a table covered in trays of bread and steaming pots, rang a cowbell repeatedly until the room finally became silent. With one final glare at the crowd, she gave a hard nod and called out.

"Tables two to nine. Line up! You can all blather on after you eat the food my team made for you!"

There were some good-natured chuckles from the crowd as the tables called rushed to line up for their supper, taking the focus off of Alex and her friends. Once the food lady was satisfied that order had been restored, she waved a server over and picked up one of the steaming pots and brought it to the raised dais. The server followed her with a tray of bread slices and they began filling the bowls set in front of each person. When they reached Matthew, he turned to Alex.

"This is my wife, Agnes. She handles all the meals here and makes a mean fish stew. Judging by the appetizing aroma, that's what we'll be eating tonight."

Alex gave her a tentative smile. "Thank you, it smells wonderful and a hot meal is very welcome after the long day we've all had." She nudged Josh who was sitting beside her with her elbow.

He nodded enthusiastically. "Yes, Ma'am. It does smell good! Thank you for sharing your meal with us. We would like to contribute some meat to your kitchen in thanks. I have a pork and a beef roast for you to add to your stores."

Agnes stern expression cracked at his words and the ladle in her hand paused as she was filling Josh's bowl.

~ 112 ~

"Beef? Pork? Oh my! It's been a very long time since we've had either of those in the kitchen. Thank you very much!"

Josh smiled back at her. "Well, we are happy to contribute it after the generosity your group has shown us with food and shelter."

Agnes nodded and moved on to fill Dara's bowl with a softer expression. "I look forward to hearing about your travels."

By the time all of the tables had lined up and served themselves, Alex and her group had finished eating. Matthew looked down the table at the group and asked, "Ready?" At their nods, he rose to his feet and whistled for attention. Once all eyes were on him and the room was silent he began.

"I would once again like to thank the talented kitchen volunteers for another tasty, filling meal. As you all know by now, we have guests with us tonight. They have thanked us for our hospitality by contributing some much-needed meat to our stores. They also bring us news of what's happening outside the city and the country. I ask you all to save your questions until they are finished telling us about their journeys."

They had already decided that Josh would do the talking for their group so he stood up and waved at the crowd with his trademark Josh grin.

"Hello, my name is Josh Green and my friends and I live in Prairie Springs. That's a small town about two hundred kilometres northwest of here. The day the lights went out, we were all on a class trip in California. Some of us traveled by land across the U.S. to get home and some of us traveled by boat up the coast and then across Washington and British Columbia to get home. We spoke to one American soldier that told us what had happened. Multiple high altitude nuclear bombs went off over North America causing EMPs to fry everything electrical on the continent, from Mexico to

Northern Canada. He also told us that the Middle East no longer exists after the U.S. retaliated.

"Everywhere we travelled was affected by the EMP. There were chaos and lawlessness everywhere but there were also communities like yours that have pulled together to survive. People who work together to grow food and provide security."

Josh had to pause when the room erupted with yelled questions until Matthew's wife rang the cow bell harshly with a glower at the crowd. Once they had settled down again, Josh continued.

"I know you have a lot of questions but I promise I'm telling you everything we know. So, here in Canada; the border guards told us that the east is a total wreck with no information coming from the government. Here in Alberta, there is some military organised and they've taken over Red Deer. What we were told was that they had no plans to come here or to Edmonton until the spring. We were in Red Deer this morning and now it looks like they won't be coming at all. They plan on expanding farming operations in the rural areas. All of this information is just rumor and second-hand info. We don't really know what their exact plans are but you shouldn't expect them to come in and rescue you." He had to pause again as the room erupted for the second time. After a few minutes, he just shook his head and sat back down. There was no point in trying to continue with the uproar his words had caused.

Matthew leaned forward to see around Alex and asked, "Did you speak with anyone in charge?" Josh shook his head but it was Alex that answered.

"Our friend Cooper enlisted and has been living with them for about seven months now. He has a better handle on what the military's plans are. He's the one who told us all about what they've been doing and what plans they have for the spring." When Matthew started to ask another question, she cut him off with one of her own. "We need to get to the hospital to search for the medications our people need. You said there are people here that could give us information about that?"

He leaned back and pressed his lips together at her interruption but then nodded at the implied quid pro quo of information.

"There is a group that went out to search the hospitals for antibiotics and baby delivery supplies. We have a few ladies that are pregnant here. One of the people who went was your friend's father. They would be able to give you more details but what they told us was that the closest hospital, Foothills was half burned out and the rest of it is filled with drug addicts. They barely escaped from there when the residents attacked them and they didn't get anything useful. They carried on to the Children's Hospital where they had much better success. All I know is that there is a group that is living there that will trade."

He leaned back and frowned in thought. Just when Alex was going to ask him another question, a group of men and women stepped up on the dais. A tall man with dark hair and a dark beard stood ahead of the others and looked them over with grim eyes before speaking to Josh.

"This group, this military group you say is controlling Red Deer, are they corrupt or are they helping the people there?"

Josh shrugged his shoulders. "From what we saw and what we were told, they seem like the real deal. They are protecting the people there and have organized housing, food and work for everyone. I don't think they are getting orders from anyone higher up, though."

The man made a face of frustration but asked another question. "So it's safe there? No gangs or attacks?"

Josh slowly nodded his head in agreement. "That's the impression we got from what we saw and heard."

Before the man could ask another question, Matthew leaned forward. "Aaron, this will be a great opportunity to explore in the spring. We can send scouts north and if it is legit, we can hopefully move the whole community there!"

Aaron scowled at Matthew and shook his head angrily. "Why would we wait for spring? We could be attacked again any day! Now's the time to get out of here!"

Josh went to speak but Matthew cut him off. "Aaron be reasonable! We don't have the vehicles to move us all that far at once. This chinook can flip at any moment so going on foot is out of the question! It would take at least a week to walk that far. People would die when the temperatures plummeted again. We must wait until the freeze is over before we consider moving."

The tension on the dais could be cut with a knife. The two men were locked in a fierce staredown with Aaron's followers grumbling behind him. Josh tried to intervene by addressing Aaron.

"Hey man, I understand how you feel but they wouldn't take you anyway. Our inside man and the soldiers manning the roadblocks at the edge of the city told us that they weren't letting anyone else in until spring. They're straining at the seams right now and don't have the resources to feed any more people. They told us to come back in the spring once they start working on the fields for planting." He tried to get through to the glaring man. "You'd probably be more comfortable and eat better here than you would there."

Aaron pinned Josh with a disbelieving glare and spoke through gritted teeth.

"It's their job to take care of us!" He moved his eyes down the table studying Alex and the other teens before he swung his gaze back to Matthew. "If these kids can do it then so can we. We're going and no one will stop us!"

Aaron whirled around and pushed through his followers, then hopped off the dais before striding into the crowd of diners. Josh and Alex tracked the angry group with their eyes as they headed out of the dining room with concern.

Matthew and Quinn spoke at the same time.

"Stubborn fools!" came from Matthew.

"They're gonna go for the sleds!" said Quinn.

Josh nodded in agreement with both of those statements. He was already bringing the walkie talking out from under the table when Alex shoved to her feet.

"We need to warn Cooper and Lisa!"

Josh and the other teens all pushed to their feet as well. Josh brought the radio to his mouth as he rose. "Cooper, come in."

The reply was quick. "Here, all quiet."

Josh's mouth flattened in a grim expression before replying.

"Not for long, buddy. We believe some people are headed your way to try and take the sleds. We're booking it back to you right now but be ready for anything!"

Cooper's voice was rock hard when he replied, "They can TRY!"

Chapter Fifteen

Cooper and Lisa closed the door of the garage behind their friends as they left to go to the dining room. The deadbolt lock on the door required a key that they didn't have so they moved a few small crates and a large toolbox in front of it to give them some security. Cooper double checked the lever locks on the overhead doors so no one could roll them up and take him and Lisa by surprise.

Once they felt secure they set up the small portable camp stove and started a pot of water to boil. Cooper had brought along a few packages of MRE's that he had been squirrelling away in the barracks so all they needed was a little bit of hot water to complete their dinner.

He was happy to stay back and guard the group's transportation and supplies with Lisa. The tension between Alex and Quinn was thick and he knew his presence was just aggravating the situation. He didn't know what had happened between the two of them but he had no desire to get into the middle of it. It had taken a long time for him to get over Alex after he moved to Red Deer and he didn't want to go through that again. He glanced over at Lisa as she laid out sleeping bags. Her expression was one of anger but her eyes were filled with misery. He understood exactly how she was feeling after the confrontation with her father. He also had two parents that had let him down in so many ways. His mom had abandoned him with a deadbeat drunk of a father that hadn't cared about him at all.

He was just about to dish up their supper when the radio squelched and Josh's voice came through.

"Cooper, no problems yet but stay frosty. I'm getting a sled envy vibe here. Over."

Cooper looked at Lisa and then nodded before replying to him.

"Frosty like ice. Watch your backs. Out."

Lisa joined him and sat down on one of the empty crates they had pulled over around the stove for seating. Her expression was still a mix of anger and sadness.

"Do you think they'll try and take our sleds?"

Cooper bit his lip, opened his mouth to speak but then just shrugged. He let out a sigh.

"I don't know. I'm sure they saw our rifles when we came in so they'd be pretty stupid to try."

She just nodded and turned away with a lost look.

Cooper hadn't really gotten to know Lisa that well before he was shot and went to Red Deer. He knew she had been a spoiled, mean-girl back before the lights went out and had gone through a major personality change just like all of them had since then. She seemed like a decent person now and he himself knew that what the world saw of a person wasn't always the true story. He didn't want to pry but she looked so sad and lost that he couldn't help himself.

"How are you doing? I mean, with the whole long lost father thing?"

Her head whipped towards him, a dark expression on her face, but that softened when she saw the genuine concern on his face. Her face went from furious to heartbroken in an instant, but her voice was filled with contempt when she finally spoke.

"What an epic fail at parenting! I mean, what kind of Dad doesn't even know what country their kid is in? He clearly didn't care enough about me before all this happened to care where I was so why not just enjoy the freedom of dumping me after the apocalypse?"

Her tone said she didn't care but the tears welling in her eyes told a different story. Cooper gave a slow nod of understanding.

"I know all about being dumped by a parent and let down by the other. It sucks. It sucks big time."

The tears finally overflowed her eyes and she dabbed at them angrily. "I hate that it hurts so much! I knew neither one of them cared that much about me but I just don't know why! What's so wrong with me that they couldn't love me?"

Cooper shook his head. "No, no, don't for a second think that this is your fault somehow! This is them being crappy human beings. Neither of our parents knows what the word family means! I really think we're better off without them. Screw them! We get to make our own family now."

Lisa wiped her eyes and nose and sniffed back future tears before nodding in agreement.

"Yeah, that's the one major thing I learned since this all happened. You don't need to be blood-related to be a family. Emily and her parents just took me in and made me one of their own. I'm so grateful to them and all our other friends for loving and accepting me the way they did. Especially after the crappy way I treated most of them before lights out. Thank God there are people in this world that are kind enough to give second chances or I would probably be dead right now!"

He gave her a small smile of agreement. "They are a pretty awesome group. I'm glad they were there for you."

She cocked her head to the side and studied him for a moment. "What about you, Cooper? Why didn't you come back? You know we all would have been happy to have you come home. There would have been a place for you just like there was for me."

He frowned and looked away before answering her. "Yeah, I know, but there's bound to be some deep scars after what my dad did to the town. Not everyone would be as welcoming as you guys." He looked back at her and raised an eyebrow. "Then there's the whole Alex, Quinn thing. Can you say awkward?"

Lisa snorted a laugh. "Uh, yeah, they managed awkward just fine without you there!"

He threw up his hands in confusion. "What happened? As much as I wanted to be the one for her, it was pretty clear that those two were destined to be together!"

Lisa nodded in agreement. "I think they still are. Quinn's just lost his way right now. His grandfather passed away suddenly from something that could have been prevented before when medication was available, and it threw him for a loop. He's lost so much with his parents dying when he was just a kid and now Harry passing. He's filled with anger at the world and it made him push everyone away. It's not just Alex, he's pushed all of us away. He wasn't even going to come with us on this trip. I think Josh basically goaded him into coming."

Cooper could understand being angry with the world. He hadn't had very many breaks himself. They dug into their meals in silence until Lisa asked about his time in Red Deer.

"It was…it felt like I was just killing time. For the first month, I was in their hospital recovering from the gunshot. I basically laid there feeling sorry for myself, getting shot, losing Alex and not being able to go home. It was a real pity party. After I got out of the hospital, they put me through basic training but I was still recovering so it wasn't really military training, more like how to follow orders training." He paused and wiped his mouth, looked down into his pouch of half eaten food and shook his head. "I wanted to help people. I don't know what I thought I'd be doing but it wasn't what I did.

"The summer months were all about farming crops. Getting them planted and tended was the biggest thing they did. The fields around town were just swarmed with refugees working but it still didn't seem like there were enough people to get all the food we'd need for the coming winter. There were teams of soldiers who traveled around the central part of the province that scavenged and brought more people back but I wasn't on one of those teams. Once the harvest was done, it switched to preserving all those crops. People were working like dogs to get everything put up before it spoiled. I honestly can't believe how hard everyone worked. It was amazing. Once that was done, we switched to stripping the city. Every house, apartment, office building and store was searched and stripped of everything that could be reused or repurposed. They have warehouses filled to the seams with shelf-stable food and goods for the future."

Lisa held up a hand to interrupt him. "Wait, there isn't a shortage of food there?" when he shook his head she frowned. "The people we saw lining up for food looked pretty thin!"

He shrugged. "They ration everything. The doctors told them how many calories people needed to survive every day and that's how the menus for the day's meals are created and served. The people might look thin and miserable but no one is starving. There's just no excess anymore. It's a hard life now and the people there aren't really happy but they're safe and they'll live."

Lisa frowned and shook her head in disbelief. "I just can't imagine living like that. Day in and day out, the same drudgery! I mean, we worked really hard on the crops and harvest too but we also had a lot of community events that were fun. At least until winter hit, then it was impossible to get out and see anyone else." She got to her feet and took his empty food pouch along with hers and tossed them into a garbage can. When she sat back down across from him she asked, "So what are you going to do after this? Will you go back to Red Deer? Do you think you'll be in trouble for leaving the way you did?"

Cooper let out a half laugh. "Honestly? I have no idea. I'm kinda hangin' in the wind here. I don't really want to go back and I'm not sure if they would even let me. As far as going to Prairie Springs with you guys, well, I don't really feel like there's a place for me there either. I just wish I had a clearer idea of what I wanted to do or where I wanted to go. I guess I just feel like I need a purpose."

Lisa nodded in agreement. "Yeah, I get that. Emily's family and our friends have been amazing to me but I kind of feel the same way. I don't exactly have a background in farming. I've never worked so hard in my life as when we were bringing in the harvest! It was actually very satisfying in a way to see all that I helped accomplish but I can't help thinking, is this it? Is this all I will have for the rest of my life? I guess it's hard to let go of what we thought our lives were going to be before all this happened. It's hard to not want more after so long of thinking we'd have more." She barked out a laugh. "You wouldn't believe how fast we all were to jump on the chance to take this trip! I guess we all feel like we need more than what the future holds."

Just as Cooper was about to answer her there was a soft knock on the door. They both bolted to their feet and rushed to grab their rifles. Cooper strode purposefully to the door and climbed on top of the tool chest before he put his ear to it. When he didn't hear anything he called, "Who's there?"

A tentative voice replied, "It's Kirkland Kelly. Lisa's dad. Is she in there?"

Cooper looked over his shoulder at Lisa and raised his eyebrows in question.

Her face had gone from wary to ice in an instant but she jerked her head in assent so he hopped down and pulled the boxes and chest away so he could open the door a crack. He glanced around her dad to make sure he was alone before opening it wider and waving him in. Once Cooper had closed and restacked everything in front of the door he turned around and let out a shout of laughter at what he saw.

Lisa's father had his hands thrust up into the air above his head while his daughter had brought her rifle up in a shooter's stance pointed at him.

Cooper took a few seconds to enjoy the entertaining view before he cleared his throat.

"Um, Lisa? We have to sleep in here tonight so if you're going to shoot him, can you take him outside first?"

Her cold as ice expression started twitching at the corner of her mouth and she just couldn't hold it so she giggled and lowered her rifle but then turned her back on the man who was her father in name only.

Cooper tried not to laugh as he walked past the man who let out a whooshing breath but his amusement faded when Kirkland said in a snooty tone, "Was that *really* necessary?"

Cooper stopped short and turned hard eyes on the man when he saw Lisa's shoulders tense up. His tone was just as hard as his eyes.

"Careful mister, she might not shoot you but I would. Be VERY careful!"

Lisa's father dropped his gaze from Cooper's and gave a soft nod before walking towards his daughter.

Lisa spun to face him. "What do you want? I think we said all there is to say."

Kirkland held out a hand to her that she ignored so he sighed deeply. "Princess, Lisa, I'm so sorry. I can't begin to tell you how sorry I am. I've let you down in so many ways. Please, seeing you here after so long made me rethink everything that I've done. I've been a terrible father to you. I'm begging you to forgive me!"

His words seemed to deflate her and she slumped down on a crate. Her eyes were sad when she looked up at him.

"Why do you even care, Dad? You got your new life here. I saw that woman. It looks like you'll have a new kid soon so why do you even care what I think? I'll be gone in the morning and you never have to see or think of me again."

His face crumpled with sorrow and his voice was choked with emotion.

"Oh Lisa, I'm so sorry. I don't want that! I don't want to never see or think of you again. This whole thing has been horrendous but it's also wiped away all the garbage that filled up our time and thoughts before. It's given me a chance to really reflect on the person, the father and husband that I was. I see now what's important and I feel like I've been given a second chance to do things better. The right way, the way I should have done them in the first place! Please, let me be the father I should have been to you. I promise I will do everything I can to make it up to you if you just give me the chance."

Cooper was leaning against the wall at the other end of the garage to give them space but he easily heard every single word spoken. He had to blink away tears. Here were the words that he dreamed he would hear from his mom one day. It had been a fantasy of his that she would swoop back into his life and beg his forgiveness for abandoning him. He swallowed hard past the knot of ache in his throat. He knew he would never hear the words being poured at Lisa's feet. He wondered what she would do with them when his radio belched static and Josh's voice flooded the garage.

"Cooper, come in."

Cooper was quick to reply, "Here, all quiet." The next words had him shoving away from the wall.

"Not for long, buddy. We believe some people are headed your way to try and take the sleds. We're booking it to back you up right now but be ready for anything!"

Cooper's eyes met Lisa's who had shot to her feet and his voice was rock hard when he replied. "They can TRY!"

She nodded in agreement and got busy pulling rifles from the trailer. Her father watched opened mouth in shock as she checked to make sure each one was loaded with a full magazine before she leaned the assault rifles against the wall by the door so they'd be easy to pass out to her friends if they needed to.

Kirkland was still looking at her bug-eyed when she finished.

"What?" She asked him.

He was looking at her like he had never seen her before. "Where, how…what happened to you, honey? I mean, the last time I saw you, you were a spoiled cheerleader who was afraid to chip a nail. Now you're all Rambo-girl?"

Lisa opened her mouth to say something sarcastic but then paused and finally shrugged and asked, "Are you the same person you were on that day?" When he looked down and shook his head she continued, "Neither am I. Bad things happened to me on the way home from California. But it was what I found when I made it home that really changed me."

His head shot up at that. "Your mother?"

Lisa let out a snort of disdain. "Oh, you don't have to worry about her, she was just fine! The apocalypse didn't even put a wrinkle into her world.

"See, a gang of very bad men took over the town and after they had killed a lot of people. They made the rest into slaves. Mom turned the house into a brothel and had most of my cheer squad working there. Not by choice, either. She was granted certain privileges for her work."

Her dad's eyes nearly popped out of his head as he sputtered in outrage. "She...you...she made you...?"

Lisa smirked. "Hell no! My friends and I showed up after that was all set up. Thank God for them. They helped me survive and showed me how real, decent people behave. Then we attacked them and kicked their asses and freed the town! The military showed up shortly after and Mom just joined up with them and left town."

She turned to Cooper. "I never did ask. How is my mommy dearest?"

Cooper grinned at her. "Oh, she's the belle of the ball in Red Deer. Reinvented herself as a victim and fell in love with one of her saviors. I'm sure it didn't hurt that he's pretty high up in command. She's a real piece of work! Claire came to see me in the hospital when I was recovering and told me if I kept my mouth shut about what I knew she had done in Prairie Springs, that she would make it worth my while."

Lisa's mouth dropped open. "Cooper!"

He let out a laugh. "Yeah, I passed!"

Lisa just shook her head. "That woman is such a..." She froze mid-sentence and lifted a finger to point past Cooper. He turned his head and saw what she had. Someone was trying to quietly lift the overhead door from the outside. It was moving up and down as it caught on the levers that latched it closed.

They both heard Josh's voice from outside the building loudly call out. "You all need to back off!"

Chapter Sixteen

Alex led her group as they rushed out of the dining room with Matthew hot on their heels. As soon as she cleared the glass doors and felt the cool night air on her face she reached under her parka and un-holstered her handgun. She cursed inside that they had agreed to leave their rifles behind. Josh caught up to her and she spared him a glance but didn't slow down when he looked down and saw the gun in her hand.

"Easy there Alex, we don't know for sure that they're making a move."

She rolled her eyes. "Maybe, but I know for sure I'm not walking all the way home!"

Alex took a quick glance behind her when she heard Emily gasp out a laugh and immediately felt better. She was too tense and Josh was right, she needed to ease up a bit. She just couldn't stop feeling angry and frustrated. Every time she tried to calm down, she saw the faces of the kids she used to babysit. The clock on their lives and everyone else that was sick at home was ticking down. The pounding footsteps beside and behind her reminded her that she wasn't alone in feeling the urgency of their task.

Matthew was out of breath when he finally caught up to them and he gasped out, "I think...you are...overreacting!"

Josh and Alex barely acknowledged him but Josh tried to explain. "The way things are now, it's better to prepare for the worst. We no longer have the luxury of giving people the benefit of the doubt."

He said this as they rounded a bend in the pathway and the garage they had left their friends and sleds in came into view. Right away they could see a group of people hovering around the overhead doors and they picked up their pace. Josh sped up even faster and as soon as he was close enough called out, "You all need to back off!"

Every head in the group turned as one to look in his direction. Josh angled towards the man door in the side of the building as the other group headed his way. He planted himself between them and the door and pulled his handgun from his holster. He didn't point it at them but he was ready to. Quinn and Alex joined him on either side and he heard Dara and Emily take spots behind them. Everyone had their handguns drawn when Matthew caught up and stepped between the two groups with his hands held out on either side of his body like he could hold them all apart.

"Aaron, please stop this! What do you think you are going to accomplish by attacking this group?"

Aaron ignored Matthew and just glared at Josh and his friends and then racked the shotgun he was holding. He had four other men with him. Two others had rifles and the other two held baseball bats menacingly. When all five of the teens raised their handguns and pointed them at his group he snarled. "They have more than they need! We just want a few of their snowmobiles to get to Red Deer before the weather turns. If they don't want to share, well then…"

As Aaron was speaking Alex could hear things being moved around inside the garage and then the door behind them opening. She kept her eyes on the threat in front of her but stepped to the side to allow room for Cooper to join them. He pointed his rifle at the other group and spoke quietly to her. "Take the rifle from my shoulder. We gave the others behind you theirs already."

She glanced his way and saw that he had brought out an extra rifle that was hanging from its sling over his shoulder. She made quick work of switching her handgun for it.

Quinn lost his patience and yelled at the other group. "We aren't giving you anything and if you try to take anything from us you'll all end up dead!"

When their only response to his words was to raise their rifles, Emily pushed through the line of her friends.

"What the hell is wrong with you? Can't you see you're out gunned? We have assault rifles. By the time you take one shot we can take twenty! Do you really want to die for nothing?"

Aaron's face was filled with contempt for her. "Please, you're just a bunch of teenagers playing war!"

Emily cocked her head at him. "Are you really that stupid? I mean, you heard our story. Do you really think we made it all the way here from California through a country that was filled with chaos and lawlessness without having to fight and kill people?" She barked out a bitter laugh. "You look at us and see a bunch of kids. Well, let me show you just how old I feel right now!"

She pulled the trigger on her rifle and a three-round burst hammered into the ground in front of Aaron and his men. The reaction from them made it clear that they hadn't been in any type of gun battle before. Aaron dropped his shotgun and stumbled backward while two of his men just turned and ran away. The other two stumbled back and fell on their butts with fear in their eyes. Emily took a few steps towards them and placed her boot on the shotgun while leveling her rifle at Aaron's face. Her blue eyes were the color of steel and just as hard. Battle hardened soldier eyes looked back at him, unflinching, and he found himself taking another step back.

"Do you understand now? Do you get that I will shoot every single one of you and just add your names to a list and then move on with my mission? Do you get it?" The last sentence was a low growl that should have never have come from such a young, sweet face.

Aaron found himself nodding his head but couldn't help but add a complaint. "It's not fair!" When Emily just raised an eyebrow, he continued, "It's not fair that you all have so much and can move around while we're stuck here!"

She kept the rifle pointed at him but lifted one hand from it to rub at her forehead wearily and then let out a sigh.

"Not fair? Do you know how many people on this continent have died in the last eight months? No? Try millions. Millions of people are dead and a lot of them starved or froze or were beaten or shot to death for the few belongings they had." She waved her hand around at the buildings. "And yet here you are, safe, warm and fed and you want to complain about how unfair it is that we have a few extra things that you don't?" She stared at him for a few more seconds before turning slightly to the side until Matthew came into her line of sight.

"Matthew, this man is a drain on your resources and you should either kick him out or kill him before he and his idiotic followers do something to put the rest of your community at risk." Her words and tone were completely emotionless and made all the more powerful because of it.

Matthew took a tentative step towards her and held his hands up in front of him. "I...I will certainly take that information to the rest of the group. Um, I think this is um, resolved now so if you and your friends want to go into the garage for the night, I can take care of the rest." His tone was soft and soothing like what you would use on a frightened animal or small child.

Emily pursed her lips like she was thinking about it and then grinned and shrugged her shoulders. "Sure! Thanks for supper and good night!"

She turned her back on Aaron and walked towards her friends, noticing their varying expressions, from shock to slight amusement. She winked and neatly slid back between them and in through the garage door.

Alex tried hard not to giggle at her best friend's performance as she turned to Matthew. He was still staring at the door that Emily had sailed through.

"Matthew, once you have this mess cleaned up, we would really like to speak to the people who made it to the hospital. I want to be away from here at first light so we need to see them tonight."

He tore his eyes from the empty door and moved them to Alex before he swung his head to Aaron.

"Um, yeah, one of the people who went is your friend's dad. So maybe you could get what you need from him."

Alex's expression turned stormy but before she could speak, Lisa put a hand on her arm.

"My dad's inside the garage, Alex. It's fine."

Alex gave her a searching look and saw that she really was fine with it so nodded and then followed her inside with the rest of the group.

Once the door had been barricaded again, they all sat around the steaming cook stove. Someone had set water to boil for drinks.

Dara was the first to speak. "Damn, Em, I almost peed my pants at how hardcore you were!"

Josh made a big exaggerated nod. "You kind of scared me a little. I thought you were going to actually kill those guys."

Emily shrugged a shoulder. "I just get so tired of everyone acting like my age is equal to my competence." She turned as if to dismiss the subject but then spun back towards the group with a scowl on her face and stomped her foot. "And for the record, I would have shot them if they hadn't backed down. I wouldn't have liked it but I would have done it!" She threw her hands into the air. "People, our people, are dying right now and even more will die if we don't get the meds they need. So, I'll do what I have to do to make that happen."

Alex stepped forward and put a hand on her best friend's shoulder. She opened her mouth to speak but then changed her mind and just gave a hard nod of agreement. She instead turned and zeroed in on Lisa's dad.

"We need some information from you, Mr. Kelly."

He squirmed a little when all eyes turned towards him but then he met his daughter's gaze and gave a slight nod. "How can I help?"

Lisa glanced over at Alex and when she got a nod, took the lead. "We need medicine for the town, for our people. Matthew said you were with a group that had gone to the closest hospitals. We need to know what we are headed into tomorrow."

He frowned at her and looked around at the others. "I don't understand why the adults would send a group of kids on such a dangerous trip if it was so important."

Alex shook her head in annoyance and stepped forward. "That's not important right now! Just tell us what you saw when you went." Her tone had a snap to it and his frowned deepened from being talked to in such a way. His expression turned indignant and he sat up straighter. Before he could speak, Lisa held up a hand.

"Dad, if you really want to help me then just answer the question!"

Kirkland Kelly sent one more annoyed look Alex's way before turning to his daughter and giving her a stiff nod.

"Fine." He let out a deep sigh. "We went just before the first snow. There are a few pregnant women here in the community and we wanted to get as many supplies as we could for the deliveries before winter set in. There were six of us. Four made it back." His eyes dropped to the ground and he rubbed at his face before continuing. "The closest hospital to us is Foothills. It's huge, with multiple buildings for different specialties. More than half of those buildings had burned out at some point but the main building seemed intact so we went there first. It was…it was a hell-scape. There were corpses everywhere. The walls, the walls were covered in blood and feces. Everything had been trashed and destroyed. We should have turned back right then but we kept going. It was the same on every floor and then we got to the fourth floor and…" He looked up at them and the horror that was in his eyes had a few of the teens shivering. "And we found, well, I guess you could call it a nest. A nest of animals that were once human. They had done things to the bodies and put them on display like some sick twisted art gallery. We just stood there, frozen in disbelief and then Andrea, she screamed. That's all it took to bring those degenerates down on us." Kirkland glanced around at the teens and shook his head in confusion.

"They were laughing. I don't know why they were laughing." He seemed to lose himself in the memories of that day until Lisa stepped over to him and rested a hand on his shoulder.

"Dad, you got away? You made it out?"

He refocused on her and nodded. "Yeah, yes, some of us did. They, well, four of us got away." He swallowed hard and continued. "We thought about going back then but if we did, it would have all been for nothing so we kept going. When we made it to the Children's Hospital, we were much more careful. Turns out we didn't have to be. It was almost in perfect condition. No one had looted or destroyed anything in it. All the doors had been barricaded shut but there were people inside. An older man came to the door and talked with us through the glass. When he found out what we were looking for, he made us wait. When he came back, he was with a woman dressed in scrubs. They moved the barricade and opened the door. We were only allowed into the lobby where the nurse talked to us and told us how the hospital was being run by her and a few others. They were friendly but cautious. We had brought some fresh food to trade so we made the deal and left. She did say we could come back if there were any problems with the babies." He looked at them all and his shoulders slumped. "That's it. We came home and I haven't left the zoo since."

Chapter Seventeen

A soft knock at the garage door had Quinn surging to his feet. He looked over his sleeping friends and saw that the knock hadn't disturbed any of them. He rubbed at tired eyes and made his way to the door in the dim light of the one candle left burning. It had been a long night of listening to gunshots and screams from across the river and he was on the final watch.

Lisa's dad had left them shortly after he had finished telling his story and they had spent what remained of the evening plotting the best course through the city to the Children's Hospital and then where to go after that. If they couldn't find what they needed there, they would be forced to move on to the next closest one and it wasn't close at all.

He reached the door and called softly through it. When Matthew called back, Quinn got to work moving the boxes and the tool chest away from the door. It was impossible to do quietly, so minutes later Cooper and Josh were there giving him a hand. By the time they got the door open and let Matthew in, the girls had gotten up and were setting up the stove to make breakfast.

Matthew nodded at them all and set a canvas bag down on one of the crates. He pulled a thermos out first and handed it to Quinn before sliding the bag's sides down to reveal a pot that had been wrapped in towels.

"The wife insisted we send you on the way with a hot meal so I have porridge and some coffee here for you."

Josh's head shot up. "Coffee? You would share coffee with us?"

Matthew chuckled at Josh's expression. "Well, don't be thinking that's a hardship for us. Coffee is something we have in abundance. The zoo had plenty in stock for their restaurants and catering department. There were also almost two hundred coffee shops in the downtown core before lights out. On top of that, we scavenged many office towers and brought it all back. Coffee is the least of our worries."

Josh shook his head with admiration. "Well, we definitely thank you for the treat and the hot breakfast!"

Matthew nodded and looked around the garage at the others. "I was thinking about your route to the hospital last night and came up with a faster, safer way for you to go." He pulled out a map of the city and spread it over one of the crates. With a finger, he pointed at their location and then the hospital. "Ok, this is where we are and this is where you need to go. The tracks you were on yesterday are in the middle of Memorial Drive. That road follows the river and would take you just south of the hospital. It's a fair hike on foot but on your sleds it shouldn't take very long. The problem is the sheer number of vehicles on that road. It was a main feeder into the core and it was rush hour when the lights went out." He looked up at them and then moved his finger a few millimeters from their position. "So, the river. For the first time in many years, it's completely frozen over so there's no reason not to use it and avoid all the obstacles on the road. It'll get you where you need to be a whole heck of a lot faster."

Quinn leaned over the map and traced the river to a spot south of the hospital. "That's perfect but will we be able to get off the river at that point or near it? How steep are the banks in that area?"

Matthew grinned. "Point McKay is very shallow. You can run up into the park there with barely a bump! Then just jump onto Shaganappi Trail and follow it straight up the hill to the hospital. Even if there's a lot of cars on that road you can go on the side. That portion of the Trail is not built up. It's just field on either side. It shouldn't take you more than half an hour, hour at the most if you take it slow."

There were smiles all around at this piece of good news. They took a few more minutes with the map and Matthew, planning the next steps of their journey if they were forced to carry on to another hospital. They plotted that route and the one they would use if they were successful at the Children's Hospital to leave the city. They all agreed that going back the way they had come into the city was a waste of time and that they would go back on the river and follow it west until they had to turn north at a town named Cochrane.

With a firm plan in place, they all dove into eating quickly and packing up. Matthew was relieved that they planned on leaving right away. After the confrontation the night before, he thought it would best that this strange group of teenagers was gone before the majority of the community woke.

He helped them roll up the overhead garage door allowing a blast of cold air in. The temperature was not as warm as it had been the day before. They all stepped out and looked up at the sky in concern. If the chinook was ending and temperatures plummeted back to what they were before they left on the trip, it could mean an even more hazardous run home.

A yell rang out causing them all to swing their gazes to the right.

"Lisa! Wait…" Kirkland Kelly was bundled up against the cold and rushing their way. He was out of breath by the time he came to a stop in front of his daughter. "So…glad…still…here!"

Lisa gave him a sad smile. "Why? We pretty much said all we needed to say last night."

He took a deep breath and reached out to grasp her hand and shook his head. "No, no there is so much more to talk about. I could spend the rest of my life talking to you, honey. But I can't do that if you aren't with me! Please, stay? Stay here with me."

Lisa took a step back in surprise.

"You want me to stay? Here?" When he nodded eagerly, she glanced around at her friends before shaking her head. "I'm sorry but this isn't my home. If you want to come back with me we could talk about that but I'm not staying here."

His expression and shoulders fell and Lisa was surprised to see a glimmer of wetness in his eyes. "I'm so sorry Lisa, I can't leave here right now. Maybe in the spring but not now."

Lisa's brow furrowed in confusion. "I don't get it. You said you wanted a second chance at being a good father so what's so important that you would want to stay here instead of coming home with me?"

He glanced behind him at one of the buildings before answering. "I'm with someone, someone I care very deeply about and…well, we're having a baby. I can't leave her and she can't travel so close to her due date."

Lisa's face was blank for a moment before it cracked into a sneer. "Well, there you have it! You got yourself a replacement family. Enjoy your do-over!"

He started to shake his head. "It's not like that…"

She cut him off with a slash of her hand. "It's exactly like that! And now that I know, I can leave and never look back." She spun around and started to walk back into the garage calling over her shoulder to the others. "Let's get going, we're done here!"

Kirkland stood dejected while his daughter's friends walked past him one by one. He received a few sympathetic glances but no one spoke on his behalf. Matthew finally stepped over to him and gave his arm a squeeze and then nodded for him to leave. There wasn't anything more he could do or say to get Lisa to stay so he turned and slowly walked away.

Matthew walked into the garage and watched as the teens loaded the last few items on their sled trailers and then he climbed on behind Quinn to take them down to the river.

The sound of engines filled the garage and then broke the eerie silence of a dead city that not so long ago rang out with sound and life every moment of the day and night.

Following Matthew's pointed directions, Quinn led them through the zoo and down a pathway that led to the river. Matthew jumped off and removed a lock on a chain link gate that blocked the boat launch and held it open as they drove through with nods and waves. He yelled out,

"Good luck!" as the last sled drove through. It was with relief that he closed the gate and relocked it. As interesting as it was to have guests and learn of the broader world, he was happy to see them go so his small community could go back to the daily fight of surviving without the drama and temptation they had brought into it.

Josh was once again driving the UTV with Dara and Lisa as passengers. He kept his eyes on the river ahead and stayed in the tracks that Quinn and Alex were making ahead of him with Cooper following in the rear. He couldn't help but shiver as they passed under the shadows of Calgary's downtown high-rises. With thousands of windows facing the river, it was hard not to feel like they were being watched by a million soulless eyes. He was so spooked that he flinched when Dara spoke. She turned in her seat and gave Lisa a penetrating look but hid the wince she felt at the lost look in her friend's eyes.

"How are you doing, hun? That must have been hard."

Lisa turned her head away from the sympathy she saw on Dara's face. The last thing she wanted to do right now was let the tears she felt pressing on the back of her eyes free. She shrugged one shoulder and shook her head.

"Whatever, it's not like he was much of a dad to start with anyways so it's not all that surprising that he replaced me."

Dara opened her mouth to dispute that but then changed her mind and just reached back and squeezed Lisa's gloved hand.

"I'm sorry. There's nothing else I can say that would make it any better. Just know that you're not alone in having deadbeat parents and I know how much it hurts, even after you think you've stopped caring. It still bites you in the butt!"

Lisa let out a small huff of a laugh at her words and then squeezed her friend's hand back.

Chapter Eighteen

The river was an excellent surface for the sleds to drive on and was wide enough that even the curves it took around and through the city didn't affect their speed by much. Twenty minutes into the drive and Quinn slowed right down until he and Alex were on either side of the UTV. Quinn pointed ahead and yelled out over the engines,

"That's the last bridge we go under. Point McKay should be just after it by a few kilometres. Keep your eyes open for the park and statue Matthew said marked it."

At Josh's nod, Quinn and Alex sped back up and took the lead. As soon as they passed under the bridge there was a gentle bend in the river and then several small islands they had to navigate around. Once past those, the river curved again and the land opened up to the north giving them a good view of a large hill. Sitting halfway up that hill was a very distinctive building that looked like it was made from giant Lego blocks.

Josh led out a laugh and pointed it out to the girls. "There it is!"

Dara squinted her eyes in that direction and asked, "How do you know that's the hospital?"

He tried to look smug. "Because I'm verrry smart!" At her disbelieving look, he just grinned. "Actually, my dad bought one of those hospital home lottery calendars and there was a picture of it on the cover. I remember thinking it was the coolest hospital I'd ever seen. The caption under the picture said that they actually had kids help design the building so it wouldn't be as scary for them to go there for treatments. Cool, right?"

Dara smiled and nodded in agreement and then pointed ahead of them where Quinn and Alex were angling towards the northern bank of the river. Josh adjusted and followed them up off the river and into a park. Except for their sleds, there was no movement in the area. They left the park and drove onto a nearly empty road that ran up the hill leading to the hospital. The higher they drove the better the view of the surrounding neighborhoods. Where there should have been smoke trails from countless chimneys and cars warming up for their morning commute, there was nothing. A city of over a million people appeared deserted.

Once they reached the top of the hill, they left the main road and cut across a field onto the hospital's property. Alex squinted her eyes and could make out three separate smoke trails rising from halfway up the side of the massive building. There was no doubt now that the building was occupied. She could only hope that they would not only have what they needed for medicine but also be willing to trade. The thought of spending the day traveling from hospital to hospital searching the ruins for the desperately needed drugs left her with a sour pit in her stomach.

They circled around the building to the front and pulled up in front of the big door frames that marked the main entrance before shutting the sleds down and dismounting. They all exchanged worried glances when they saw the gleam of safety glass scattered across the snow. It had to have been recent that the windows were broken or the glass would have been covered by the last snow fall. Someone had made an attempt to cover the empty frames in the door with what looked like metal shelving but there were still gaps around the frames.

Everyone took a quick step back when a double barrel of a shotgun slid smoothly in between one of those gaps to point at them.

"You all can just climb back on those machines and hightail it outta here! There won't be any warning shots this time, I promise!" The voice that rang out was furious. When the teens just shot looks at each other the voice got louder. "You bunch ought to be ashamed of yourselves! Attacking a house of children and tryin' to steal from kids. I should just shoot you all dead right here and now!" The barrels jabbed towards them making Alex flinch but Josh threw up his hands.

"Mister! Hey, Mister! I can see you had some problems here but I can assure you that it wasn't us. We came to trade. A group over at the Zoo sent us here to trade!"

There was silence on the other side of the door and then some mumbling Alex could just make out.

"Hmm, the zoo? The zoo people? Right, right, they came for baby supplies. Skittish bunch, had trouble over at Foothills..."

To Alex, the voice sounded like an elderly man that was either going senile or was very tired. She reached up to unsnap her helmet strap and then pulled it and her toque off, letting her hair spill down around her shoulders. She took a short step towards the doors and called out.

"Sir? I'm sorry for your troubles but we aren't here to cause any. We traveled a very long way to find the medicine our people need. Do you think you could help us? We have supplies we can trade if you can."

There was silence from the other side of the barricade for half a minute while the group held their breaths, hoping for the right outcome. The barrel of the shotgun stayed steady on them even as he replied with a softer tone.

"Trade we can do but don't think for a moment I wouldn't put a load of shot into you all at the first sign of funny business!" The barrel jabbed in their direction causing them all to flinch before it pulled back and disappeared. "You all just stay put out there and I'll go fetch the boss."

There were sighs of relief from every one of the teens and they all relaxed slightly. As they waited for the man to come back they removed all their head gear and talked quietly about the trade.

"How much food are we willing to trade them if they have what we need?" Quinn asked.

Alex snorted. "All of it!" At Quinn's frown, she shook her head in exasperation. "If these people have what we need then we give them everything we can to get the deal done. Do you really want to haggle over the little bit of food we brought when it could mean more of our town dying? If we can get what we need here and not have to travel anywhere else in this city, then we should just make it happen."

Quinn nodded but looked away making Alex want to throw up her hands in frustration. She was so sick of his stubborn, combative attitude. There were a definite time and place for it, but this wasn't it.

Josh put a hand on her shoulder. "You're right Alex, but let's keep that close to our chests for now. We don't know what the setup is like here so we should keep a few cards up our sleeve until we do."

She kept her gaze on Quinn for a few more seconds and then sighed in frustration and turned away when he wouldn't look at her. One thing that would come from this trip was the resolving of their relationship. As much as she wished they would get back on track, he was proving that it wouldn't happen and she should just let him go. She knew eventually they would have to talk about it. It just wasn't in her nature to leave something so big unresolved.

It only took a few more moments before they all heard movement behind the shelves blocking the door and then a different voice rang out to them.

"Hello? Al says you're here to trade?"

Josh was surprised to hear a woman's voice but he quickly nodded at Alex to take the lead. She took a step towards the door and raised her hands in a peaceful gesture.

"Hi! We were told by a group living at the zoo that you are open to trades. We traveled here from up north looking for medicine. There are a lot of sick people in our town and we hoped to find what we need here."

There was silence for a few moments and Alex could see someone giving her group a closer look through a small opening between the frame of the busted-out door and the shelving blocking it. When the woman's voice called out again, Alex had to try hard not to let her eyes roll at the same old question.

"Where are the adults? Why would they send a bunch of teenagers?"

Alex shrugged. "They didn't. We wanted to help our people so when the chinook hit we just decided to come here. Hopefully you have the medicine they need."

There was no reply right away but the teens could hear sounds of a conversation happening on the other side of the door. When Alex heard the man's voice rise up with "A bunch of kids!" she hoped that they would relax enough to deal with them. They all shared a hopeful glance at one another and then turned back to the door when the woman called out to them.

"We are willing to talk about trading but before we let you in, you need to leave all your weapons outside!"

Alex ground her teeth together in frustration but before she could reply, Quinn called back to the woman.

"No offence ma'am, but based on the broken windows and what your man said about an attack, that's not an option." When his words were met with silence, he huffed out a sigh. "We really don't mean you any harm but we've travelled a lot in the past eight months and being without a weapon now is suicidal. There are a lot of really bad people out there but we aren't them. We just want to trade you some good farm food for some medicine and get back to our homes. We aren't looking for a fight!"

There was more hushed conversation on the other side of the door before they all heard sounds of furniture scraping against the floor. The shelving unit was pulled away from the door and a woman stepped into its place. Her face was tired looking but her expression was hard as she looked them all over. She finally gave them a nod and focused on Quinn.

"I understand your concern but you must understand mine. We are responsible for the lives of sixteen children. I can't just let a bunch of strangers with rifles into our home and hope for the best."

Alex moved forward. With the way Quinn had been acting lately, she didn't want his bad attitude to put the woman off and sour any chance at getting a trade done.

"Ma'am, I completely understand where you're coming from. I would do the same in your place. Would you be open to just two of us coming in, unarmed, to discuss a trade?"

Quinn's head snapped in her direction and his voice was a bark. "ALEX!"

She rounded on him and stabbed a finger in his direction and spoke through clenched teeth. "Not...one...word!"

When he broke eye contact with an angry shake of his head and turned his back to her and the woman, Alex returned her gaze to the woman. She had taken a step back into the doorway at Quinn's harsh tone and now her expression was wary. Alex held up a placating hand.

"I'm sorry. He's just very protective."

The woman glanced quickly at Quinn before cautiously nodding her head. "Yes, I would be ok with that."

Alex sent her a small smile before turning to the others. "Josh, Dara?"

In response to the silent question, Dara and Josh both lifted the slings of their rifles over their heads and passed them to Emily and Lisa. They walked towards the front doors with their hands out in front of them to show they were unarmed. Alex let out a relieved breath when the woman nodded and stepped back for them to enter the lobby of the hospital.

Once they were gone from sight, Alex turned and scanned the surrounding area for any threats. Cooper, Emily and Lisa fanned out and did the same. She tensed when Quinn took a step towards her. He didn't speak for a few moments.

"I know you want to get the trade done Alex, but sending our friends in there unarmed?"

She sent him a scathing look before focusing back on the surrounding area. "Yeah, that would have been pretty stupid. Good thing they both have handguns under their parkas!" She shook her head. "I know you don't think much of me anymore but I'm not an idiot. Try and remember that at least!"

She caught his flinch out of the corner of her eye. "Alex, I don't..."

Alex narrowed her eyes at a glimpse of movement on the edge of the massive parking lot. She cut Quinn off and started to back up.

"Contact! There are people out there!"

Quinn swung his head to his right and started backing up too.

"There's more in this direction too! We need to get inside. We're sitting ducks out here with no cover!"

Alex spun around and bolted towards the lobby door causing the man who was standing in it to raise his shotgun. She was right about him, he was at least seventy years old.

"Mister! Are you expecting company? There's a bunch of people headed this way!"

His expression changed from confused to fearful when he stepped out onto the sidewalk to look past her.

"It's those buggers from yesterday! They want in to steal the drugs!"

She came to a halt when the barrel of his gun swung back towards her.

"Whoa! We aren't the enemy! We can help you fight them off but not from out here. We need some cover to get behind. If you let us into the lobby we will hold them off until you can get the rest of your people in place."

The man studied her for a few seconds and then looked back out at the threat heading their way. His shoulders drooped and he seemed to deflate before her eyes.

"I have no choice but to trust you. There aren't any other people to get into place. It's just me and Leslie left, plus the children."

Alex felt her jaw drop at his words. How could these two ever protect a building this size from the evil out there? She shook her head. Doesn't matter now, work to be done! She spun back to her friends.

"Guys! Get the sleds moving, we need to bring them into the lobby!"

As she ran towards her sled, she could hear the old man bellowing into the hospital for the others to come back. Throwing a quick look towards the parking lot as she fired up her sled, she saw at least fifteen people headed their way. The quick glance showed that they all were carrying what looked like bats or crowbars. If that was all the attackers were armed with then they shouldn't have any problem taking them out. She barely had that thought when a gunshot rang out and she saw the snow fly up not two feet from the front of her sled. As she gunned the sled towards the now open lobby doors, she hunched her shoulders waiting for the bullet that she feared was coming her way.

Chapter Nineteen

Alex, Emily and Cooper managed to drive their sleds into the huge lobby with Lisa hot on their treads with the UTV. They all managed to get inside without getting shot thanks to Quinn who stayed back and laid down covering fire. He burned through two magazines on full auto before diving in behind them. Josh, Dara and the woman they had gone with came running back towards them and lent a hand getting the shelving back in front of the door. They added desks and pieces of wood to the growing pile as well. Once Quinn had caught his breath, he looked around the dim lobby in confusion before zeroing in on the woman.

"Lady, you need to get the rest of your people down here to help defend this place!"

She shot him an annoyed look and turned towards the barricade.

"Yeah, that would be helpful. Too bad there is no one else. It's just me and Albert left now!"

Quinn started to sputter in surprise but was cut off when Cooper thrust a handful of spare magazines his way.

"Here, reload! How many do you think you took out? How many are left out there?"

Quinn shook his head as he ejected the empty magazine from his rifle and inserted a full one.

"I don't know. I saw at least six or seven go down but it might have been more. I was just hoping that the spray would get them to give up and retreat." He turned to the old man who was looking out at the lot between the shelf and the frame of the door.

"Albert? How many do you see out there?"

The older man grunted, turned his head and opened his mouth to answer when a shot rang out and he flew backwards off his feet. Quinn's mouth gaped open in shock as he watched the man hit the cold tile floor. Albert's arm flew out to the side and the butt of the shotgun he was holding slammed down beside him. He must have had his finger on the trigger because it belched out the shot in the chamber. The sound was deafening in the enclosed space and they were all lucky the barrel was pointed off to the side or they all would have been injured from the spread of the pellets.

Most of them had instinctively dropped to the ground when the shotgun went off. Cooper had been facing Quinn so he didn't see Albert hit the ground but he did see Alex slam violently against the wall as she caught part of the shot in her right shoulder. He watched as if in slow motion as she flew forward and then toppled back. He didn't hear the noise of her head cracking against the floor but his brain imagined it.

Cooper shoved Quinn to the side and scrambled on hands and knees over to her while screaming her name. His voice was lost in the barrage of automatic gunfire as Josh, Dara, Emily and Lisa poured fire from their rifles around the barricade. He gathered Alex into his arms and lifted her. Keeping his head down as low as he could he shuffled towards the back of the lobby as fast as he could with her dead weight in his arms. He slid into the dark doorway of an empty café and gently laid her back down, quickly checking to make sure she was still breathing. When he found that she was, he jumped to his feet and ran around the counter of the café and pulled dish towels from a shelf to use as padding for her head and to put pressure on her shoulder wound.

He had just turned her on her side to apply pressure when the woman, Leslie, dropped to her knees beside him. He looked at her desperately when she took the towels from his hand.

"GO! I'll take care of her!"

Cooper shook his head harshly. "I'm not leaving her!"

Leslie grabbed his shoulder and gave it a shake. "I'm a trauma nurse, I know what to do here. They need your help out there! GO!"

Cooper stared at her hard for a few moments before giving a reluctant nod and with one last look at Alex's blank features, pushed to his feet. He rushed back out into the lobby and did a quick scan. Everyone was still firing their rifles around the barricade except Quinn who was still on his knees. His gaze was fixed on the small pool of blood that Alex had left on the tile from where she had landed after getting shot. Cooper raced towards him and roared Quinn's name breaking him from his fixation with the blood. Cooper had no choice but to ignore the utter devastation in Quinn's eyes when he looked up at him. Hauling him to his feet, Cooper shoved Quinn towards a hallway to the right with signage pointing to the parkade. They needed a better look at the parking lot and the attackers than what they had if they were going to end this attack.

Quinn stumbled ahead of him, constantly looking back towards the lobby until Cooper grabbed him by the shoulders and shook him.

"Snap out of it, man! She's alive and the nurse is fixing her up. We need to get a bead on these bastards and take them out or we'll all be dead!"

Quinn took a deeper breath and steadied himself when Cooper said Alex was alive and being looked after by the nurse. He pulled away from Cooper and straightened his shoulders. His expression hardened.

"I'm going to kill them all!"

It was said so coldly that Cooper took a small step back but then nodded and waved Quinn on. They followed the dark hallway for a few feet to a corner and looked around it. The hallway turned into a section that was all glass on the outer wall, flooding it with light. The double glass doors to the parkade were twenty feet further on. They would be exposed to the parking lot the whole way. When Quinn only hesitated for a few seconds before charging forward, Cooper groaned but followed quickly behind him, keeping an eye on the lot through the windows. He could see five attackers still on their feet and many more laying lifelessly on the snow-covered pavement. The ones that were still up were using abandoned cars and an empty cement fountain as cover while they took shots towards the barricaded lobby doors. Thankfully none of them were looking their way.

They made it through to the open-air parkade and crouch-walked towards the end of it until they were slightly past the attackers. They rose up until they could see over the cement half-wall and did a scan of the area to look for any other attackers than the five they had already seen. A faint scream reached them from inside the hospital causing them both to abandon their search. In unison, both boys rose to their feet and started firing into the sides of the men that were shooting at the doors, being careful not to aim towards the barricade themselves.

All five attackers were down in less than a minute. The boys dropped back down behind the cement half-wall and waited for any return fire. After a few nerve-racking minutes when none came, they cautiously raised back up. There was no movement and only silence from the parking lot. Both their rifles jerked towards a piercing cry coming from one of the downed attackers but nothing came after it. They waited again and then Quinn nodded towards the lot.

"Let's go out and take a look."

Cooper scanned the area and the gauged the distance one more time before nodding. He followed Quinn out of the parkade towards where most of the bodies lay. The first body they came to made Cooper flinch and quickly look away. It was a woman and the expression she died with was ugly. Her face was skeletal and covered in open sores that gleamed wetly in the daylight. They both backed away from her and continued on to the other bodies. Each one they came to had similar infections covering their exposed skin. They kept a healthy distance from the bodies after that and neither one made any attempt to touch them or the discarded weapons they had fought with. Whatever had been wrong with these people the boys didn't want to take a chance on catching it. When they confirmed that all the attackers were dead they turned and backed away to the barricade.

Cooper called out, "It's clear out here!" but received no reply. He shot a concerned glance to Quinn before trying again. "Josh? Girl's?"

The only reply he heard was the sound of distant crying. Quinn rushed over and they were about to run for the parkade when they heard sounds of furniture being shifted. The shelving unit started to slide back so they helped move it from their side until there was enough room to squeeze between it and the door frame. Josh's pale, drawn face greeted them. He looked past them at the bodies in the parking lot and shook his head with a grim expression before moving out of the way to let the two boys in. The first thing Cooper and Quinn saw was a fresh pool of blood on the tile floor. It was on the opposite side of where Alex had gone down so they knew that another one of their friends had to be shot.

When the three of them shifted the shelves back into place, Quinn reached out and touched a bullet hole at waist height that had light shining through it. He turned his head towards Josh and whispered, "Who?"

Josh looked away and slammed a booted foot into one of the shelves shoving the whole unit flush with the frame before letting loose with a string of curses. He finally wound down and scrubbed at his face before turning back to his friends.

"Lisa was hit in the side. The lady nurse is working on her and Alex. The old guy is dead."

They all turned and looked towards the back of the lobby as a pained cry rang out and then slowly walked towards their injured friends.

Chapter Twenty

Alex's eyes fluttered open and the light shining on her face caused a spike of pain to fill her head. She squeezed her eyes shut again until she could get a handle on the ache and then cautiously opened them a crack. The first thing to come into focus was a pair of big owlish grey eyes that were framed by lush black lashes. She stared at the eyes until they blinked and a giggle erupted. The eyes belonged to the small thin face of a little girl who reached towards Alex's face and gently touched one of her golden red curls. The small monkey face whispered, "Pretty" before it dropped under the level of the bed and disappeared.

Alex was confused and wracked her throbbing brain for the last thing she could remember. All she could think of was being in the Children's hospital lobby and being kicked in the back, then…nothing. Without moving her head, she let her eyes scan the area of the room she was facing and saw another bed beside hers. There was a person lying on it and after squinting, she could make out that it was Lisa. Seeing her friend was either sleeping or unconscious, she tried to reach for her, causing a new explosion of pain to blossom on her back shoulder. Alex couldn't help the groan of pain that poured out when she thrashed her head to the opposite side and squeezed her eyes closed against it. The scrape of wood on tile had her eyes flying back open in search of a threat. Instead, she found Quinn's grief-ravaged face looking back at her.

His eyes were filled with so much pain and anguish that she feared the worst. Her voice was barely a croak when she forced out, "What happened?"

His face crumpled even more but a few deep breaths had him partially composed. He stood and stepped towards her bed before taking her hand.

"You were accidently shot by the security guard when he was shot at the barricade. His weapon discharged when it hit the floor and you caught some of the bird shot pellets in the shoulder. Leslie, the nurse, says that it's ugly but not life threatening. She was more concerned with your head. You hit it pretty hard when you went down. There was nothing she could do but hope that you woke up. Without diagnostic scans, there was no way to tell how bad it was."

Alex scrunched her face up in annoyance at being taken out of the fight so quickly but was more concerned for the rest of her friends. She swallowed painfully against the dryness of her throat and mouth and asked,

"Lisa? Everyone else?"

Quinn's eyes flashed over to the other bed before coming back to rest on hers. "Lisa was shot too, but by one of the attackers. Leslie says she was very lucky that it was a through and through and didn't hit anything critical." He tried a wobbly smile. "Lisa disagrees on the lucky part!" The smile faded. "The guard, Albert, died instantly. All the rest of our friends are fine, just worried about you and Lisa."

Alex closed her eyes. They had been through so much and faced so many dangers that they were incredibly lucky that they hadn't lost anyone in their core group. Mason had died after being shot on the road by the gang that had taken over their town, but he hadn't been a close friend. She knew they took risks that most people wouldn't these days, but she also knew that none of them regretted anything. Sitting back and letting people die just wasn't in any of their natures.

"Alex?"

The sorrow in Quinn's voice had her opening her eyes again.

"Alex, I don't even know how to ask for your forgiveness. I've been such an ass these last few months." She kept her expression blank as he struggled to find the words to express himself. He finally turned away and pulled the chair he had been sitting in towards her bed and settled heavily into it before he spoke again. "When Grandpa died, I just shut down. Losing one of the most important people to me after everything we had gone through to get back to him, well, it enraged me. I was so furious at the world and him. If he had just told me he was out of medication…Anyways, I just lost all reason. First, my parents were taken from me and then him. The only thing I could do was push everyone away so I wouldn't hurt like that again." He took a shaky breath and lifted his head to meet her gaze. His eyes were welled up with tears and his voice broke. "When I thought I had lost you this morning, I realized how stupid I've been. Instead of pushing the ones I love away, I should have been holding them close and cherishing every moment I could have with them."

Alex tried her best to keep her expression neutral but she had longed for him to say these very things for so long. Her heart was pounding to reach for him but her head was cataloguing all the damage he had done with his actions over the past months. She quite wasn't ready to let go of the hurt. The only thing she could do at that moment was to turn her face away from him so he wouldn't see the conflict in her eyes. She heard him sigh sadly.

"I don't know if you can forgive me or if we can ever get back what I threw away but I hope you'll give me the chance to make it up to you."

The silence was thick as Alex blinked away the tears that were trickling out of the corner of her eyes across her temple and into her hair. Her eyes focused on Lisa who was watching her from the bed across from hers. When the silence dragged on, Lisa rolled her eyes, nodded towards Quinn and made kissy motions. A small smile tugged at Alex's lips until she finally gave a small nod and turned her head back towards him. He had his face buried in the palms of both hands. She opened her mouth to speak when the door to the room swung open and a woman Alex had only met briefly walked in. She stood at the end of Alex's bed with her hands on her hips, her head swinging back and forth between Alex and Lisa.

Alex thought the woman looked like she hadn't slept in days. Her pallor was almost grey with exhaustion and her eyes looked hopeless. The strong, no-nonsense tone that came from her countered how she looked.

"Good, you're both awake!" She drilled Alex with a look. "Your head must be awfully hard to come through that hit!"

Her expression softened slightly to a smirk when Lisa snorted and mumbled, "You have no idea!"

Leslie turned to Lisa and asked, "What number from one to ten would you give your pain level?"

Lisa lifted one shoulder in a shrug. "I don't know. Maybe a five? I mean, it definitely hurts, but it's nothing compared to when you were cleaning and stitching it up!"

The woman nodded. "Good, let me know when it creeps up to eight or nine. That'll mean you're ready for another pain med dose." Her head swung back to Alex and she raised an eyebrow.

Alex shook her head but winced at the spike of pain it brought. "Sixty-three!" She uttered through gritted teeth. "But I don't want any medication. My head's fuzzy enough without it!"

The woman came up beside the bed and reached under it. The whole upper portion of the bed tilted upwards until Alex was in a sitting position. The movement caused nausea and she was forced to take quick deep breaths to stop herself from puking into her lap.

"Yup, definite concussion there. Just give yourself a few moments for it to settle and no quick movements. I'm Leslie by the way. I patched up your shoulder. Had to pick eight pellets out from under your skin. You were very lucky you only caught the edge of the shot spread or you might have lost your entire arm or your life. I'm not quite set up to do major surgery anymore." When Alex just kept deep breathing, Leslie patted her leg. "Don't worry, you'll have minimal scarring and should be able to use that arm for light duty in a week to ten days. You just have to give it time to heal. The head on the other hand…well, concussions are tricky. Based on the way you flew forward and then back to the floor, you probably have a case of whiplash as well. You'll have pain, dizziness, light sensitivity and maybe nausea for at least a week to ten days. Symptoms can persist off and on for a few months. The good news is, you're young and relatively healthy so you should bounce back faster."

She glanced around at Lisa and then Quinn before frowning. "Actually, all of you are the healthiest people I've seen since this all began. Where did you say you guys come from and what's the price of admission?"

A voice from the doorway had Alex's eyes popping open.

"The price is all the plague medicine you have."

Emily stood in the doorway with Cooper hovering behind her. Her expression was one of relief to see Alex sitting up and awake.

Leslie cocked her head to the side in confusion before her expression morphed into fear and she took a step back from Alex's bed. Emily stepped into the room shaking her head.

"Not us! Our town. We all live on farms surrounding the town. With the extreme cold, none of us has been in there for months. The town quarantined itself and put up barricades over a week ago when the first cases showed up. They've been dying ever since. We left yesterday to find medicine." She looked around the room at her friends before looking back at Leslie. "We brought food to trade. Beef, pork, eggs and some preserves. You can have it all if you have what we need to save our town." She held out the piece of paper with the names of the medications Dr. Mack had said he needed.

Leslie hesitated but then reached out and took it. She read the short list over before looking up at the teens.

"I have all of these here in the hospital." She frowned thoughtfully. "BUT, I don't know if there's enough for a whole town of people. Actually, I doubt there would be enough, and if they can't treat everyone there, then most likely there would be more cases flare up."

Alex groaned and closed her eyes but not before she saw the grim look on Emily's face. She heard her friend speak in a harsh tone.

"Dammit! That means we have to go to another hospital!" When no one responded, she swore angrily. "We didn't come all this way and have two of our people shot just to give up now!"

Alex sighed and opened her eyes to reassure her friend that they wouldn't give up when Leslie spoke again.

"I might have a solution for you...but...I have a few questions for you first." When she received nods from the teens she asked, "These farms you all live on, are they safe? Do they have a good supply of food and water?"

Emily looked to her friends before cautiously nodding her head. "Yes, everyone is well armed and security is taken very seriously. We also all have fully functioning farms with livestock and crops. We are in very good shape to make it through the winter and planting season until the next harvest."

Leslie studied her for a moment and then seemed satisfied she was telling the truth.

"Final question. Would your people or families be willing to take in strangers?"

Emily's shoulders dropped and her face went cold. "You want in? Getting tired of having to take care other people's kids?"

Leslie's mouth dropped open in shock and she gasped. "What? NO! God, I would never abandon my kids! I want you to take some of them back with you. I...I can't leave. I have to stay here."

An uncomfortable silence filled the room once again until Emily stepped forward and put a hand on a weeping Leslie's arm.

"I'm sorry. It's such an ugly world we live in now. My first instinct is always the worst of people. Please, will you tell us what you're thinking? How did you end up here with so many kids?"

Leslie went and pulled a visitor's chair from the corner of the room and wearily dropped down into it. She rubbed the tears from her tired face before looking at Cooper.

"Your two friends downstairs will keep watch?" When he nodded his head yes, she seemed to deflate. "Then let me tell you what hell looks like."

Chapter Twenty-One

"That day, that hellish day, I personally saw eight parents commit suicide. I'm positive there was more but I saw eight do it that day. Within an hour of the power going out, ninety percent of the kids on the critical care floor had died. By the third hour, the rest were gone. The neonatal unit…" She paused there and just shook her head in disbelief. "When I left that floor, I knew God had left us all." Her face was haunted by the images she'd never be able to erase.

"It happened first thing in the morning so most of the staff was in house for the day shift. We worked like dogs to save them but with no electricity, no equipment? Anyways, we had no idea what was happening out in the city. We heard people talking about all the cars and trucks that had stopped working but it wasn't until after the first die off that we stopped and really heard what everyone was saying. They said that planes had just dropped from the sky like paperweights. It wasn't until I climbed the stairs to the roof and saw all the smoke trails that I truly understood that it was over. I saw people that looked like ants all over the major roadways walking while all motorized vehicles were at a standstill.

There were other people up on the roof with me looking out at the dead city. When the first man and woman jumped while holding hands there were screams of horror. By the time I left the roof, three more people had followed them." She leaned forward, put her face in her hands and scrubbed at her eyes like she was trying to scrub away the memories. Leaning back in the chair, she continued.

"I found parents who had taken their dead child's morphine drip and used it to overdose. Others found different ways to do it. It was like they all just gave up and wanted to be with their kids. As bad as that was, it was the kids that didn't have any family in house that I found the hardest to bear. Some parents would have been at work or home and had no way to make it to the hospital. Some of the kids were from out of town and had no one near to come for them. Whatever the reason, they were here, scared, sick, in pain and alone.

"Most of the staff stayed the whole day but when the next shift didn't show up, they started to trickle away. Can you blame them? They all had family out there somewhere, kids of their own to find. But those of us left had to deal with floors filled with dead patients and scared alive ones. Parents were screaming for us to do something but there was nothing we **could** do! Nothing worked! All that lifesaving equipment was useless. The elevators wouldn't work to take the bodies to the morgue. The refrigerators didn't work anyways. No one could get the generators working and, and…NOTHING WORKED!"

Leslie leaned back in her chair and tipped her head back to stare blankly at the ceiling, lost in the memories.

"By the next sunrise, seven more patients had died and parents started to pull their kids out. They took every wheelchair and even a few stretchers. I have no idea if they ever made it to their homes. More staff had left in the night leaving only six of us. Two nurses, one doctor, one security guard, one woman from catering and one orderly. We went floor by floor and collected all the patients and family members and brought them all down to the cafeteria. It was just too hard to have everyone spread out and, well, the bodies…

"There were thirty-six patients left and eighteen family members. We made a plan and just got on with it. What else were we going to do? Twenty-four adults can get a lot done when they have no choice. It took days, but we managed to get all the bodies out of the hospital. We didn't have a way to dig a big enough hole so we were forced to burn them." Her voice dropped to a whisper. "All those little bodies with no one to stand for them. That… that day almost broke me." Leslie cleared her throat, rolled her head on her neck and went on.

"Albert was such a strong voice. He seemed to know what was coming and he guided us on so many things. He was a widower and lived nearby. He wasn't even here that first day. He showed up first thing the day after the power went out with a hunting rifle and shotgun over his shoulder. He organized a group of the fathers and they set off to the nearest grocery store. They pushed empty laundry carts to the store and filled them to the brim with non-perishables. One of the fathers told me later that Albert shamed every person that tried to stop them by telling them that the food was for the sick kids at the hospital. He told anyone that would listen that the kids had been abandoned there to die. He said it was amazing to see angry mobs fighting over canned goods stop at Albert's words and help fill the carts." She laughed softly. "I'm sure it helped confirm his story that all those carts have 'Property of Children's Hospital' stamped on the canvas. Anyways, that was Albert, he could talk his way around anyone. He probably saved us from being raided at least a dozen times with words instead of bullets. He would spin his story of abandoned children that should be allowed to die in peace and comfort and they would just turn away." Tears sprang into her eyes and she dashed them away. "I'll miss him so much. He made me believe in God again."

"So, we just went on. They went to a plant nursery and found seeds and we planted a garden around the playground. A few parents finally made it here and took their children away. Some of the kids finally succumbed to their cancer or other diseases they had been fighting and some of them healed enough to try and travel with their family members back to their homes. I wish they had of just stayed. From what we can see from the roof and what our scavenging parties saw, there were no homes to go back to. But one by one they left and the family members of children who passed left too, until it was just me and Albert. Then the first snow came and something strange started happening. We would find boxes of canned food or stacks of firewood in front of the lobby doors. People remembered or they heard Albert's story and they tried to help when they could. It was an amazing feeling knowing that there is still good out there. But it also caused something else to happen. People saw this place as a sanctuary for children and when they ran out of food and hope they brought them here and left them. I guess they thought they would have a better chance of surviving here than out there in the city. Some of them have come back for their kids and some of the kids were old enough to run away to try and find them again. Right now, there are sixteen children here. Eight of them will never leave here. They all have either a terminal disease or complicated medical issue and quite frankly, I have no idea how they've lived this long. The other eight are healthy, well, as healthy as near constant starvation allows. They have no one in this world but me, now that Albert is dead. I just don't know how I can keep them all alive by myself." She turned her head and met each teen's eyes. "So, I know exactly where you can find the medicine your town needs in large quantities but I need a big trade for that information."

Alex was the first to speak. "You want us to take the kids home with us."

Leslie nodded and then bit her lip waiting for a response.

Alex sniffed back the last of her tears from hearing the woman's story.

"I want to take the kids home with us. But we can't. We don't have room to transport them on the sleds. I'm so sorry."

Leslie's face fell but her head and everyone else's swung to Cooper when he spoke. "Yes, you can. I'm not going with you."

Before anyone could process his words, another voice spoke up. "Neither am I. I'm staying here." They all turned to see Lisa sitting up with a determined expression on her face. "Also, I'm sitting at a solid thirteen so I'll take that pain pill anytime please!"

Leslie pushed herself to her feet and slid out of the room as the teens all started to talk at once.

Emily rushed over to Lisa's bedside and helped to lower her back onto the bed. "Lisa, why? Why would you stay here?" The room quieted as everyone wanted to hear what she had to say.

Lisa scanned each of her friend's faces and gave them all a sad smile. "You are all my family. You took me in and helped me be a better person than I ever would have been in the old world. I can't tell you how grateful I am to each and every one of you. But, my Dad, he's here and as much as he has to account for, he can't do that if I'm miles away. Also, I'm going to be a big sister so I have to be around to make sure he or she doesn't grow up to be a jerk like I did! You guys gave me the first real home I ever had. You showed me what it means to be a family so now I have to show him and the only way I can do that is if I stay here in the city."

Emily had tears dripping down her face but she was nodding her head in understanding and so were Alex and Quinn. Alex turned her gaze from Lisa to Cooper.

"Cooper?"

He gave her a beautiful, happy smile. "This is my place." At Alex's confused look, his smile just got bigger. "Prairie Spring's is not my place and Red Deer isn't either. I keep feeling lost. I want a place where I can help and do something worthwhile. This is it. This is my place. I'm not going to leave a single woman here all alone with eight sick kids to try and feed them and keep them safe. This is where I'm supposed to be. One day I might head back your way but right now, here, this is where I'm supposed to be."

Alex opened her mouth to argue but then closed it. There was nothing she could say to dispute his reasoning. That's what all of them wanted. To do good and help others where they could. Cooper had found his place so she just returned his big smile with one of her own and nodded her head in agreement. She had to hold back an exclamation of surprise when he turned to Lisa and shot her a wink. Maybe this was his place in more than one way.

Quinn came to stand by her bed and took her hand. "I'm still not sure we can fit eight kids. I guess it would depend on how big they are."

Leslie stepped through the door with two tiny paper cups in her hand. They had pain medication in them and she insisted Alex take hers. Once she was satisfied both her patients were taken care of, she turned to Quinn.

"None of the kids are very big. The oldest is ten and I'd be surprised if he weighed over ninety pounds."

Quinn thought about it for a minute and then motioned Cooper over. "Hey, can you go swap out Josh? I need to talk logistics like weight and gas issues with him."

Cooper nodded and turned to leave but hesitated and then turned back to Quinn and Alex.

"You know how I said that this is my place? That this is where I'm supposed to be?" At both their nods he grinned. "Well, you two found your place a while ago and it's not Prairie Springs…it's with each other. Whatever happened, let it go. Don't lose your place." With that, he turned and left the room.

Chapter Twenty-Two

Josh came stomping into the room with Dara close behind him. He scowled at the girls and focused in on Quinn.

"What the heck, man? I go on guard shift for a few hours with my lady and our people start leaving the Scooby gang? What did you do?"

Quinn held up his hands in defense but said nothing so Josh swung his gaze over to Lisa. He made his voice sound hoarse with an Italian accent.

"Don't you know that no one ever leaves the Mafia? Once you're in, you're in for life!"

Lisa just smiled indulgently at him as Dara shoved him out of her way and went to sit between her and Alex's bed.

Josh shook his head at no one appreciating his humor and turned to Alex. "Hey there, Red. Good to see you awake but you're looking a little woozy. You ok?"

Alex blinked a few times at him and tried to smile but the medication was taking hold and she felt herself slip away.

Josh blew out a worried breath at her reaction and turned to Quinn. "Is she going to be ok?"

Quinn nodded. "Yes, she just needs some rest. Leslie gave her some pain killers so they probably knocked her out." He brushed an errant curl from her face before asking, "Cooper fill you in?"

Josh rolled his eyes. "Sure, we came with seven, lost two and gained eight. No prob, piece of cake!"

Quinn sighed and looked away. "I know but is it doable?"

Josh looked over at Lisa and the other girls before answering. "Well, short answer is...yes."

Quinn raised his eyebrows in question. "So what's the long answer?"

"The long answer is I'm leaving my sled here for Cooper and Lisa. I understand their reasons for staying but I'm not going to leave them without transportation. Or protection for that matter, so they keep the rifles and we dump at least half of the ammunition we have left with them. We're giving them almost all the food we brought as well so that lightens us up a lot. We have the two sleds and their trailers and the Ranger that will tow the third trailer. Alex isn't going to be able to drive so that puts her and the driver in the UTV. Depending on how small the kids are, we can put three in the back of it too. Not comfortable but it can be done. Two of us on one sled with a kid in between on the bench. One of us and two kids on the bench of another and that leaves two kids left. Only other place for them is on one of the trailers."

Quinn winced. "That's not very safe, is it?"

Josh snorted. "What the heck's safe anymore? We'll bungee cord them down to it or something!"

Quinn shook his head in amusement. "Or, one of *us* in the trailer with one kid to keep them in place - while bungee corded in. Then two kids on the bench of the other sled with one of us driving."

Josh gave a sharp nod. "Deal!" He looked down at Alex's sleeping face and frowned. "What kind of timeframe did the nurse give you before Alex can be moved?"

Quinn blew out a breath. "Well, she said it could take a few weeks for the concussion symptoms to go away but they might take longer. Her arm shouldn't be used for at least a week to ten days."

"We both know Red's not going to wait that long to head home. She's going to insist we leave in the morning. As much as I don't want to aggravate her injuries, we might have no choice. There's a bit of bite to the air outside. Not as bad as it was but it's definitely getting colder. If the hard cold hits us again before we get home, well, we just might not make it home at all."

Quinn turned and walked over to the window. They were on the third floor so he had a pretty good view of the sun inching closer to the mountains as it got ready to set. At best, they only had two hours of daylight left. He turned back and saw Leslie enter the room with a large paper bag. She walked over to him and Josh and held it out.

"This is all the stock I have of the two medications that are effective in treating the plague."

Quinn just stared at what now seemed to be a small bag. "How many doses are in there?"

She swallowed hard. "Thirty courses total."

Quinn's shoulder's drooped but he nodded. "Ok, so where do we find more?"

Leslie bit her lip and looked away while she answered him. "I just need a guarantee that you'll take my kids somewhere better. I can't just trust..."

Quinn's face filled with anger but it was Josh who spun towards her.

"Lady, we are leaving a tonne of food, ammunition to protect you and two of my very good friends with you as well as a snowmobile. Even if this place you send us to has burned to the ground, we'll STILL take these kids out of here to our homes! What else do you want, a contract in blood? Fine, go get your vampire pokers and get on with it!" He spat out while holding out his arm for her to draw blood from.

She looked up at him in surprise. "Two of you are staying? What?"

Josh dropped his arm and huffed out a breath.

"Yes, Cooper and Lisa are staying here with you. Cooper wants to help protect you all, now that your friend has died. Lisa's dad lives at the Zoo with a community there so you might want to consider joining them for even more security." With her expression filling with hope, Josh softened and reached out again, this time to pat her arm. "I promise, the kids are going with us. They'll have more than enough to eat and warmth and love from all our families. Please, tell us where we need to go."

With tears of gratitude in her eyes, Leslie told them. "There's a central distribution center for all medications in Calgary. They made all the deliveries to every hospital and all the pharmacies in the city. Even if they've already been looted, it probably would only have been for the narcotics but I doubt they've been hit. There's no sign saying what's in there and it was a very secure building. The only problem is that it's on the other side of downtown. That's somewhere I wouldn't want to go through."

Josh was already digging the map of the city from an inside pocket of his parka. He spread it out on the floor and looked up at her.

"Show me."

Once she had shown them the location, Josh leaned back against a wall and tapped his lips with his finger as he thought it out. He finally gave Leslie a hard look.

"You know you can't stay here any longer, right?"

She sadly nodded her head. "We should have left a long time ago. We just didn't know where to go."

Josh leaned over and tapped a spot on the map. "It's just not possible to go it alone anymore. These guys seemed like decent people to me, except for a couple of blowhards, that is. They have security, heat and they grow food year-round."

She nodded slowly. "Ok, but why would they take on eleven more mouths to feed?"

Josh grinned. "Because what they'd be getting is worth much more than food." At her confused look, he explained it to her. "They will be getting a trained trauma nurse, all the medication and supplies that you still have here, two soldiers with automatic weapons and a functioning means of transportation. Also, the food we give you will sweeten the pot. They don't have a lot of meat and that's mainly what we brought with us."

Leslie leaned back on her heels with a wistful smile. "Sounds great but how am I supposed to make this magical deal with them and move all my kids and supplies there without getting jacked along the way. Also, what's that got to do with you guys going to the distribution center?"

Josh fell back against the wall. "One, you aren't going to make the deal. I am. Two, we will transport you, the kids and the supplies there on the river. Three, the Zoo is over half way to the distribution center building so that's where we leave from in the morning. Four and five…we're going to need a lot more gas and finally…it's going to be a really long night!"

Josh looked up when a shadow blocked the light from the map to see Dara standing there with her hands on her hips and a frown on her face. His face split into a cheeky grin.

"Hi honey, can I go out to play?"

She shook her head in annoyance and stepped to the side so Emily could join them with a matching frown. Emily pointed at the map and barked out, "Break it down! How does this play out?"

Josh gave her big exaggerated nods of his head. "Yes, ma'am! First," He turned to Leslie. "Are there still lots of cars with gas in your parkade?"

She nodded. "Yes, the second and third levels haven't been touched yet."

Josh beamed at her. "Perfect, there's our gas station. Ok, Cooper, Lisa and I go back to the Zoo, like pronto! We sell them the deal and when they fall all over our feet in thanks, we radio you guys and then you and the love of my life bring the sleds, the trailers loaded with all the kids who are staying and Leslie riding double with one of you." Leslie's expression turned to objection, but before she could speak Josh held up a hand. "Stop, the trailers will be padded with a kazillion blankets. Four kids to a trailer, all laying on their sides, all tucked in tight. We'll secure the tops with more blankets and then use bungee cords to keep it all in place. It's the only option other than doing the trip ten times and that's NOT an option." When Leslie spread her hand in a continue gesture, he nodded and went on. "Once you are there, we will leave Lisa and Cooper with you and then Emily, Dara and I head back here to get all the supplies that you want to take and will have made ready for us to load up. We will then bring those supplies to the Zoo and stay there for the night. Just before first light, Cooper, Emily and I will head to the building to get the meds. After that, we drop Cooper off back at the Zoo and come back here to load up the rest of the kids and go home. All that matters is that the river stays frozen and hopefully empty."

He leaned back and gave a half bow but then threw his hands in the air at the scowls being sent his way.

"What?" He asked in annoyance and pointed at Quinn.

"So I'm just supposed to sit here while you all go running around the city?"

Josh cocked his head. "Good point. Ok, you come too and we'll leave an injured Alex and eight little kids to fend for themselves." Quinn glanced over at a sleeping Alex in concern before stepping back with a small nod so Josh turned and pointed at Dara.

"Why am I not going to help break into the medicine building? Why do I have to stay at the zoo?"

He again cocked his head to the side. "Good point. Ok, you can come too and we'll leave an injured Lisa, Leslie and eight sick kids there alone and hope that group doesn't double cross them now that they have a bunch of supplies, ammo and one of our sleds. We'll just pick them all up from off the river where they'll be thrown and bring them back here. OR…keep them honest with your big daddy boom stick until Cooper can get back to watch over them."

She stuck her tongue out at him but stepped back so he turned and pointed at Leslie but before she could let loose he pre-empted her.

"You're going to have to just trust us. You and the kids go before the supplies so that you already will have a place there. We don't want your supplies and we aren't going to steal them so just let it go. The kids will be bundled up and safer than we will be in the trailers. I promise we will go as slowly as possible to keep them safe." When her mouth snapped shut, he raised an eyebrow. "Is there anything else?" When she just glared at him, he sighed and put a hand on her arm. "Leslie, this is the only way I see this happening. We could just go get the meds and leave you, Cooper, Lisa and the kids here but I think we both know that the sanctuary image that was protecting this place is now gone. There is just no way the three of you can defend this place on your own. You have to go. Either we take you or you wait and try walking there. Do you think that's doable?"

Her glare shifted to one of frustration and then resignation before she gave a small shake of her head and looked away. Josh gave her arm a squeeze and then looked up at his friends.

"All right, let's get to work."

Chapter Twenty-Three

While Alex and Lisa slept and recovered from their injuries, the rest of the teens started to prepare for the next steps in their mission. They all knew that they could have just taken the medicine Leslie had offered and went home with the hopes that it would be enough to save their people. The risks they were about to take to help the nurse and the children from the hospital as well as the dangerous trip to the distribution center could result in more of their numbers being injured or worse. After talking it over, they all agreed that Josh's plan was the right course of action and worth the potential risks.

Josh and Quinn headed down to the lobby and pulled all of their gas cans from the sled trailers. They topped up all the gas tanks with what remained in the cans and then loaded the empties onto metal food service carts before pushing them out and up the ramp into the parkade. Josh had come up with an easier way to get the gas from the dead cars. Siphoning the gas with a hose was a difficult and time-consuming task on newer model vehicles so they bypassed it completely by placing a hospital bed pan under the actual tank and using a screwdriver and hammer to just puncture a hole in the tank itself. The gas flowed out, filling the pans, and then was easily poured into a funnel and into the gas cans. Josh crawled out from under a truck and stood to brush the grime from his snow pants.

"I don't think you guys should stay here in the hospital after we leave for the Zoo. There's no way you would be able to defend a building this size by yourself if it's attacked again."

Quinn poured the lasts drops of gas from the bed pan he was holding and turned to his friend.

"I agree. I was thinking about that too but we are running out of time. We can't spend hours looking around the area for a smaller, safe location and then transporting Alex and the rest of the kids. The more we run our sleds, the better chance someone will hear the engines and come to investigate." He screwed the cap onto the can and pulled an empty one from the cart. "I was thinking, maybe one room in the basement we could block off so we're all in one place. Hopefully, if anyone comes looking tonight, they'll stay out of such a dark place and just search the rest of the building for loot. It might be better to hide than fight at this point."

Josh nodded and walked over to the next parked car. "I think you're right. We can run it past Leslie and see what she thinks."

When Josh slid under the next car, Quinn turned and looked back at the main hospital building. He couldn't keep the concerned expression from his face when he thought about how they were going to get through the night and then make it home with eight little kids that he hadn't even met yet. He wondered how the girls and Leslie were doing. The three of them had gone to speak to the children and explain what was about to happen. He wished them luck with it. Telling a bunch of kids that they would be split up from the family they had made and moved away from the only home they had known since the disaster was going to be difficult, to say the least.

Emily and Dara stood outside the partially closed door to where Leslie had made her and the children's home and listened to her explain what was about to happen. They both cringed as a few childish angry voices rang out followed by multiple cries of denial. When more than a few of the kids started to wail, they both backed up down the hallway. Dara lifted her hands and shoved them into her hair.

"My God, I feel like a baby snatcher! How can doing the right thing feel so wrong?"

Emily winced at a piercing cry and shook her head. "I know but the bigger question is how do we transport them home if they're fighting us the whole way? I totally understand how awful this is for them but if they don't go along with the plan, they could be putting all of them and us in danger." She blew a sharp breath towards her forehead to blow hair out of her eyes. "Someone's going to have to be bad cop."

Dara raised an eyebrow. "Really? Do you honestly think you can bring the hammer down on a poor orphaned kid that's bawling its eyes out?" She shook her head. "I know I won't be able to!"

Emily shrugged. "I bet Alex could. She can bring the "Don't mess with me" tone out on anyone."

Dara huffed out a laugh at that understatement. "Unfortunately, I think Alex isn't going to be at her best for the rest of this trip. It'll have to be one of us. It can't be one of the boys or it will just scare them."

Emily screwed her face into a cold scowl. "Sit your butt in that seat and close your trap or you're walking the rest of the way!" Her tone and expression changed back to normal. "How was that?"

Dara nodded her head slowly. "Not bad. Very annoyed Alex-like."

Emily shrugged. "We'll just have to do our best. We'll be as nice and understanding as possible but feelings and comfort will just have to take a back seat until we get home safely. Once there, the Moms can hopefully take over." She groaned at the thought of her parents and what their reactions would be when they finally did get home. Maybe she could convince Josh to pull an RV over to Alex's and she could just live there. It might be safer!

Her thoughts were interrupted when the door was pushed open, letting a wash of end of the day sunlight into the hallway. Leslie beckoned them with a pinched expression. They both took deep breaths and plastered on reassuring smiles before walking through the door. When sixteen small, sad and angry faces looked their way, Emily couldn't help but think she would rather face off with armed raiders. Dara raised her hand and gave a cheery wave.

"Hello, everyone! My name is Dara and this is my friend Emily. We are very happy to meet all of you!"

Her introduction was met by stony silence until one of the boys looked to Leslie and begged, "Please don't make us go with them!"

Dara's face filled with uncertainty when she looked around the room and saw more little faces turn to plead with Leslie.

"Uh..." She stammered out when suddenly Emily cut her off.

"What's this? Make you?" She said in an outraged voice. Waving her hand in the air in dismissal, she gave the boy and then all the others a hard look. "We aren't here to make anyone come with us! We are here to conduct interviews for personnel who would be suitable for a huge adventure!" Silence and confusion greeted her declaration. She strode towards the boy who had first objected and stabbed a finger towards him. "You! You look like you know what you're doing! Tell me, how are your tractor driving skills?"

His mouth dropped and he shook his head. "I...I can't drive a tractor!"

Emily's face showed shock. "What? Well, we would certainly fix that! It's an important skill for a young man. How about your aim? You can shoot a slingshot, correct?"

He looked around at his friends with a small smile tugging at his lips before he answered her. "No, I've never had one."

"Unacceptable! Every young man needs to know how to drive a tractor, shoot a slingshot and build a tree fort in the woods!"

She turned away from his growing smile and strode towards three little girls all huddled together. Two of them had blond hair and one had brown. Emily guessed their ages to be around five or six. When she stood before them, they looked up at her with big tear filled eyes.

"Hmm, you three look experienced to me! You do know how to deal with chickens, correct?"

The girl's eyes seemed to get even bigger and they shared quick glances with each other before shaking their heads.

Emily threw her hands up in the air. "How is that possible? It's like the biggest treasure hunt...ever! First, you must toss handfuls of seed all over the ground and while the chickens run around bobbing for seeds, YOU run around collecting all the eggs. It's very technical!" She made chicken pecking motions with her body and head as she explained it. Once she saw small smiles growing, she changed track and scanned the room. "Ok, I know you all know how to care for horses, right? No one? Ride horses?" When all the children were shaking their heads, she spun in a circle with her hands on her hips. "Well, tell me you could at least manage to have wagon rides pulled by horses?"

At least half of the children nodded their heads and bounce in their seats. Emily looked them all over and tapped a finger against her lips in thought. She turned to Dara.

"I'm not sure. None of them seem to have many adventure skills. It would be a lot of work to show them how to do all of those things. What do you think, Dara?"

Before Dara could answer, a girl with dark brown hair, around nine years old pushed herself to her feet and took a few steps towards them. She gave them a hopeful look before dropping her eyes to the floor.

"I would like to learn about chickens and horses but..." Her eyes flashed back up quickly before dropping again and her voice was hesitant. "Do...do you have food...food and heat? We...we haven't had much food and it's hard on the little ones and...and I'm so tired of always being cold."

Emily heard Leslie start to cry behind her as she knelt down on one knee. She beckoned all the kids to come forward and sit on the floor around her. Once they had all settled, she reached behind her and gently pulled Leslie in to complete the half circle.

"I know things have been hard here. Leslie and Albert did everything they could to take care of all of you. You've all heard that Albert died today?" When they nodded their sad little faces, she went on. "It's very sad but he died doing his favorite job...taking care and protecting you all. Before he died, he said he wished you could all live somewhere safe and warm. That's one of the reasons we want to help you all. Leslie can't take care of you all here in this building by herself and she wants you all to be safe and warm.

"So, let me tell you about where we live. My friends and I all live on big farms around the town of Prairie Springs. We all have huge old farm houses with lots of bedrooms. Our big kitchens all have wood burning stoves and so do most of the rooms. The furnaces that heat our houses run on a gas called propane and we all have generators to make them work with enough of that gas to stay warm for the rest of this winter and hopefully all of next. There are a lot of people there who work to take care of each other and lots of moms and dads." Emily had to suck in a breath at the awe on their faces when she said moms and dads. She tried to clear her throat of the emotion but struggled with it. Thankfully, Dara jumped in.

"Food! So much food! We worked all summer long helping to grow massive fields of food. When it was time for the harvest in the fall, there were mountains of it! There was so much food that we filled all the cellars and storerooms and there was still too much so we shared it with all our friends who live in the town. So! You will be warm and you will eat three times a day, every day. Everyone will have a family and there will be board games and card games and books to read every night after supper. As soon as the snow melts, your adventure training will begin and by the end of summer you will all know many new things. Your skin will be golden brown from the sun with super strong legs from running and playing outside all day." Dara noticed some of the kids looked even sadder than before and remembered that not all of the kids would get to live on farms.

"The Zoo! How could I forget? They have some really cool stuff there too. They have these huge glass buildings where it's always warm inside and so many gardens filled with food that grows all year round. Inside those buildings is like summer all the time. I bet there are butterflies fluttering all over those buildings, even during the winter!" Dara was relieved to see the kids who were going there perk up and start to smile.

Emily and Dara answered a flurry of questions from the kids. Emily noticed the girl who had asked about food and heat slide back out of the circle and move to a corner of the room. She pulled a sheet of paper from under a cot and brought it back over to Emily. Her little hands shook as she held it out to Emily. She took it from the girl and looked it over. It was a drawing of two horses running in a field with a forest in the distance. The girl's voice was wistful.

"Does it look like that at all?"

Emily grinned up at her. "It looks very much like that!"

Her grin faded when she saw a tear slide down the girl's cheek and she whispered, "I would have really loved to have seen that."

Emily shook her head in confusion as the girl took her picture and went back to her cot. She turned to Leslie for an explanation. Leslie's eyes had tracked the girl to her cot and were filled with sadness.

"That's Anna, she will be going with me to the Zoo." At Emily's look, she sighed. "Anna has Cystic Fibrosis. She needs to be watched over very carefully and the medications she needs won't last much longer."

Anger flashed across Emily's face. "Then why didn't you tell us you needed more? We're going to the distribution center! We can get everything she needs there, can't we?"

When Leslie's eyes widened in realization, Emily threw up her hands.

"For heaven's sake, Leslie! Make a freakin' list of everything you want and we'll bring it back for you!"

Leslie dropped her head. "Yes, of course. I'm sorry! I guess I was just so resigned to the idea of all the meds running out soon, that I didn't even think about getting more. I will! I'll make a list for you to take."

Emily nodded and looked back towards Anna but then had a thought.

"Wait a minute, can't CF be managed at home? I had a friend whose brother had CF and he seemed fine most of the time. Medication, inhalers and certain exercises helped him manage it so he could lead a pretty normal life."

Leslie nodded. "Yes, with the right instruction and medication it can be managed. Many kids lead relatively normal lives now."

Emily glanced at Dara and then back to Leslie in confusion. "Ok, so then why can't she come with us too?"

Leslie laughed in disbelief. "Seriously? You're taking eight kids as it is. Eight more mouths to feed and care for. I didn't feel I could ask you to take another that needs so much more!"

Emily raised a mocking eyebrow. "Then you're an idiot. Anna is exactly who should come with us. Every single thing we do now is work. What makes it worthwhile is love and happiness. She might be more "work" but that just means all the more love and happiness, for her and us. Start making a second list of everything I need to know about CF management or find me a book or something. That kid is going to ride a damn horse!"

Dara and Emily pushed themselves to their feet and left the room while most of the kids chatted in excitement about life on a farm. The others talked about what living at the Zoo would be like. They had only made it a few steps down the hall when they heard footsteps behind them. It was the boy who didn't know how to drive a tractor. He came to a halt in front of them and shot a quick look over his shoulder to make sure they were alone before speaking.

"I can't go!" His face was set in a very determined expression.

Emily spread her hands. "Why?"

His lower lip quivered slightly but he bit down on it before he spoke again. "I promised Albert! He was teaching me things, like how to do a patrol and what to do if we were raided. He said if anything happened to him, I was to take his place and help Miss Leslie with the smaller kids. I have to stay with her!"

Dara stepped forwards and placed a hand on his shoulder. "What's your name?"

"Aiden."

"Aiden, Leslie really wants you kids to come with us. She knows what's best for you and you should do what she wants."

He shook his head. "Who's going to look out for her? Do you know why only eight of us are going with you? It's because the other ones are sick and they're going to die...soon. It's not fair that she has to stay with them alone for that! I should be there with her to help. And I made a promise!"

The girls looked at each other lost in how to reply. This brave little boy just wanted to do the right thing too. How could they force him not to?

Before they could come up with anything to say, Josh came around the corner bringing the faint smell of gasoline. He planted a kiss on Dara's cheek and asked,

"We get everything sorted out on who's going where?"

Aiden spoke up in a firm voice.

"I'll be going to the Zoo to look after Miss Leslie and the sick kids!"

Josh nodded and stuck out his hand for a shake. "Alright! Good to have another man on board to help out!"

The kid's grin split his face. After a quick shake of Josh's hand, he whipped around and disappeared back into the kid's room.

Josh was grinning, pleased with himself on handling the kid when he turned around to see Dara and Emily glaring at him.

"What?" he asked innocently.

Chapter Twenty-Four

Josh asked Leslie to join them in Lisa and Alex's room but when he went through the door and saw the fury on Alex's face he strongly considered making a run for it.

"NO! NO chance in hell, you're all going to leave me here and go tearing around this city!"

Josh winced but slid partly behind Dara for cover and let Quinn take it.

"Alex, be reasonable! You're in no shape to go anywhere yet. You need more time for your head to settle."

Alex glared at Quinn and then threw her blankets back and sat up to get out of bed. They all saw her face drain of colour before she started to sway. Quinn reached out to steady her just as she turned her head and threw up all down the side of the bed. He helped her lean back against the pillows and grabbed a towel to help clean up the mess.

Josh judged it safe and stepped around Dara and further into the room.

"So, I think that clears up Alex's participation tonight!"

Alex groaned out a few curse words and Dara hammered him in the arm with a punch before going to help clean up the sick. Josh rubbed the ache in his arm before turning to Leslie.

"Quinn and I were talking about a fallback location. We don't think the ones who stay back here would be safe in the building with just Quinn on lookout. Is there a place nearby or in the building that they could hide out and defend if necessary?"

She frowned at him but nodded then walked over to check Alex's eyes and bandage. Once she finished with Alex, she crossed over to Lisa to check hers.

"Albert prepared a place for us to go if we had to evacuate. We can go there. Or, I mean…Alex, Quinn and the kids can." She blew out a breath. "I can't believe after all this time I'm going to lose them." She looked down and repeatedly smoothed the sheets over Lisa's leg.

Josh cleared his throat. "Not necessarily." When all eyes swung his way, he held up his hand. "Cooper and Lisa will be with you and after...err...when you're ready I mean, it would be a good idea for all of you to head back to our place." Everyone looked away when they realized he meant when the sick children all died. "The Zoo is a good fix for the rest of winter, but now that they know about Red Deer, I would guess at least half of them will bolt there as soon as the melt comes. There's just no way they can sustain the place and guard it against all the crazies they say are still running around the city if they lose that many people. Lisa should try and convince her dad and his girlfriend to come too. I've already given Cooper my take on it and he agrees. He's going to look for another trailer for the sled or some other means of transport so you can all head our way right before the snow melts. The other option is to wait and find bikes for all of you. However you do it, don't stay after people start leaving."

Lisa nodded from her bed but Leslie seemed unconvinced so he left it at that. There was only so much he could do.

"So, where is this fallback Albert set up? The sun's about to drop behind the mountains and we need to start moving."

Leslie patted Lisa's leg one more time and turned to Josh. "It's right across the parking lot. The Ronald McDonald House. We don't think anyone would bother with it. If they come all the way up the hill, they'll go straight for the hospital, at least at first. We'd have time to get away while they search this place."

Josh turned to Quinn who raised a shoulder in a shrug. "Yeah, that makes sense to me. Raiders would go straight for the drugs and medical supplies in the main building. We'll just keep a low profile and it should be ok."

Josh nodded and looked to each of his friends. They were about to split up and spend the dark hours of the night in possibly dangerous situations. They had learned the hard way today that they weren't invincible and any one of them could be injured or worse. He took a deep breath and squared his shoulders. All trace of goofiness now gone.

"Everyone still in?"

As one by one, his people gave firm nods of commitment, his nerves got tighter but it didn't stop him from nodding himself.

"Go time."

Coming Soon….

Sun & Smoke, Book Three in the Endless Winter series.

-And-

Read on for an excerpt from Iced, Book Six in the Stranded Series

To be notified of every new release, sign up for my New Release Newsletter at

www.theresashaver.com

You will only receive an email when a new book is coming out!

Also by Theresa Shaver

The Stranded Series

Land – A Stranded Novel
Sea - A Stranded Novel
Home - A Stranded Novel
City Escape - A Stranded Novel
Frozen - A Stranded Novel

Endless Winter Series

Snow & Ash
Rain & Ruin

http://www.theresashaver.com/books

Excerpt from: Iced - A Stranded Novel

By Theresa Shaver

The woman stumbled when the toe of her boot caught on the crusted snow of the drift she was trying to navigate. She felt herself falling face first towards the snow-covered ground but was saved when both of the men she was traveling with grabbed her arms from either side and steadied her. She sent them both a weary smile for the help and looked ahead past the snow-filled field to the cleared road. Walking would be easier once they reached it. Her calves and thighs burned from the unaccustomed exercise but she ignored it and focused on being grateful for the chinook that brought the arctic temperatures up to survival levels and allowed them to escape from the death trap their home had become.

When the town council had posted notices on every door of a forced quarantine, she had been slightly relieved. The sickness burning through the population terrified her. Knowing that they would now be forced to stay away from others, locked in their homes, gave her a sense of protection. Every time she or any of the others that lived with them went out, there was a fear that they would bring the sickness back with them and infect everyone in the house.

It was the same day the notices went up when one of their roommates started to cough. That barking noise had frozen all eight of them with terror. Food and water were hastily gathered by each of them and then they all went to separate areas of the house in hopes of isolating themselves from the contagion.

The two men who chose the basement rec room with her were long-time friends from before the lights had gone out and had been kind to her from the start as they settled into the new living arrangements. They divided the basement room into three quadrants, settled in and then waited to see what would happen with their sick roommate. They passed the time bundled under blankets to stay warm and talking about things they missed from the old world while trying to stay calm about their situation. All three were losing the battle when on the second day, the basement door was opened and a voice yelled down to them.

"Two dead, two more sick! If you are all still healthy, don't come up!"

All three of them looked towards the ceiling with fear. How could this infection move so fast? People were dying just a few short hours after symptoms appeared.

One of the men finally yelled back, "We're all fine down here but we will run out of food and water in the next couple days."

There was silence from the top of the stairs for a few minutes and then a thump on the steps could be heard before the voice called down again.

"I've left you some supplies on the steps. Wait until I've closed the door before coming up to get it. Good luck!"

The door slammed shut and the three stared at the steps leading to the main floor. The man closest to the stairs threw back his blankets and pushed to his feet. He stood at the bottom of the stairs looking up in thought. He eventually turned back to his area and rooted around until he found a spare shirt that he tied around his face like a mask. He climbed the stairs slowly until he was high enough to reach out and snag the cardboard box that rested on one of the top stairs and then made a quick retreat back down. He set the box on a desk by the stairs and turned to look at the other two.

"One at a time we can come take what we need. As long as we stay at least ten feet apart, we should be ok."

When they both nodded their agreement, he reached into the box and took a few items before carrying them back to his area. The woman went next and then the other man. They were all relieved that they could now stay in the basement for a few more days without having to go up for more supplies and risk infection. None of them considered that the supplies might have the deadly germs on them. None of the roommates realized that the last supply run to the community hall had been done by the roommate that had first come down with the illness and that he had brought the infection into the house. They didn't consider that the ones he had infected had also contaminated the supplies in the kitchen.

It was the next day that they started talking about escape. She posed the question first.

"What do we do if they all die up there? We can't stay trapped down here. We'll run out of food and water, not to mention the cold! If no one's left to keep the stoves going then the little bit of residual heat we get will disappear and we'll end up freezing to death."

There was silence from the two men before one of them started nodding.

"She's right. We have to get out of here. We should leave and move into one of the empty houses."

The other man shook his head. "That doesn't solve the supply or heat issue. We'd have to go to the community center for everything we need to survive and that just exposes us to another chance at infection."

It was another hour before the woman spoke up again. "We need to get out of this town! The council said the farms haven't been exposed and they were still bringing food to the roadblocks so we could go there and ask to be taken in until this passes."

Hope flared on the men's faces until reality set in. "We would never make it. The temperature is just too low to survive the walk."

She threw up her hands in frustration. "So, we stay here and die or try to leave and die? If that's all we can hope for then I say let's go while we are still strong enough to have a chance of success." Her declaration was greeted with nods.

On the fourth morning since the plague had come into the house, they dressed in every piece of clothing they could find in the basement, pried open a frozen window that sent a small avalanche of snow into the room and one by one crawled out into the front yard. Two things greeted them.

Utter silence and lack of movement in the neighbourhood, and a much warmer temperature than they expected. They worked their way through the walkways and alleys, trying to keep out of sight until they reached the first open field. Half way across it, two of them started to sweat with fever but chalked it up to exercising in so many layers of clothing. The cold and exercise had them all thirsty and they went through the little water they had brought quickly, so when they started coughing they assumed it was due to thirst. None of them ever entertained the thought that they might also be sick as they trudged towards the distant farms.

David Perry leaned his back against the gate blocking the main driveway of the Green farm and adjusted the sling of the rifle over his shoulder in annoyance. Everything seemed to annoy him since his friends had left the day before to find medicine. He just couldn't understand why they would want to throw themselves back into the danger they all knew was out there. Making it home from California after the lights went out had been a terror-filled journey, not to mention the battle to free the town. At least they hadn't had to do too much once the first group of adults had been freed. The adults had taken over the fight and he had stayed out of it.

David knew that most of his friends had been forced to kill others in self-defense but he was lucky enough not to have been put in that position. He kicked at the softening snow under his boot and thought about the look of pride in Mr. Green's eyes when Josh told him they were going to search for medicine. Josh's dad hadn't even objected once to his son running off to play hero. David just didn't understand. Why couldn't some of the men go instead of a group of kids? When Alex and Emily's parents had shown up yesterday in a panic after they discovered that the girls had gone too, there had been a full-blown argument between the adults. When Alex's brother weighed in on the side of the teens, David was furious. Here was a former police officer giving his approval of their quest and he used their experiences crossing the country to justify that they stood a good chance of succeeding.

In David's opinion, that was one of the biggest reasons that they shouldn't have gone. They had been through enough already. Why couldn't they just stay safe and let the adults handle things? He didn't want to be a soldier. He had seen the effects of that with his father and how it had destroyed his family. The hardest part of not agreeing with his friends was the distance it was creating between him and Emily. She wasn't interested in his opinions on the matter and every time he brought them up she would just dismiss his concerns without even trying to listen. She hadn't even said goodbye to him when the girls had picked up the trailers they were going to take with them. Just a quick wave and then she was gone without a backward glance.

He shook his head and shoved himself off of the gate. Was it really so bad that all he wanted was to stay here with his mom and little sister? To just be safe and not have bullets flying at him or have to shoot people? He just wanted to live his life as close to how it used to be before the lights went out. He didn't think that made him a bad person.

He was so deep in his thoughts that he didn't hear the crunch of snow under boots coming from the other side of the fence. It took the bark of a cough and a voice calling out for him to spin around in surprise.

"Thank GOD! We didn't think we would make it!"

David's eyes widened in surprise at the three people approaching the gate but it was the way the trio staggered and swayed that had him taking a step back in concern. When the woman between the two men doubled over with a coughing fit, his concern turned to fear and he took three more steps back and held up his hands.

"Stop! Don't come any closer! Where...why did you come here?"

The taller man looked past David at the farmhouse with glassy eyes. "We need help. I worked for Mr. Green during the harvest." His eyes tracked back to David. "Do you have any water? We ran out halfway here."

David spun around and searched the yard for someone to help him but there was no one in sight. He spun back when he heard the chain on the gate clang against the metal post. All three had moved up against it and one of the men was trying to unwrap the chain that held it closed.

David's heart was pounding in fear when he asked, "Are you from town?"

The woman gasped out a breath against another cough and nodded. "Yes, we had to get away. Everyone is dying! Please, do you have water?"

David shook his head violently. "You're sick! How could you bring that here? You're going to infect all of us!"

The woman was shaking her head in denial when the sound of the front door to the house slamming shut rang out. He was filled with relief that one of the adults were coming to help. That relief turned to terror when his little sister, Emma's voice called out.

"Davy? Are we having visitors? Did they bring any kids to play with?"

David was frozen in fear when one of the men raised his boot and put it on the middle cross post of the gate to pull himself up so he could climb over. He finally found his voice and screamed out, "Stop! Emma, get away from here!"

He could hear her small footsteps squeaking in the snow as she moved closer. When the second man raised his foot to the gate to try and climb too, the words Quinn had fired at him in contempt when they talked about sick people showing up, flooded his mind.

"It's no different than them pointing a gun at our family!"

Too much was happening at once. Emma was right behind him asking who the people were. Both men had reached the top of the gate and the woman was doubled over again in a coughing fit.

There was nothing he could do. They were going to kill him and his sister and everyone on the farm.

The strap of his rifle slipped down easily with a jerk of his shoulder letting the gun drop into his waiting hands. He breathed out and whispered to his sister, "Close your eyes."

As he pulled the trigger at a distance where he had no chance of missing the three from town, he closed his own eyes.

To be continued...

49923812R00117

Made in the USA
Middletown, DE
24 October 2017